Dr. Allen had his back to her, but there was something about his stance which tugged at the corner of her mind.

It was when he turned around.

"Hi, Dr. Walton…"

The words died in his throat, whereas Ingrid felt as if the world had dropped out from beneath her feet. She stood there stunned, like a deer trapped in a set of headlights, as she stared into those light cerulean eyes which had the darkest rims around them so that they seem to make the blue of his irises pop.

It was the eyes which had attracted her to him in the first place. The only difference was that his dark hair had grown out. It had been buzz cut the last time, but he hadn't spiked it as he'd threatened to do all those months ago. That had prompted a discussion on cheesy pickup lines, which had then deteriorated into her sleeping with him.

He'd also aged a bit—but then war could do that to a person. Still it was him. Clint. The soldier who had taken her virginity. The man she'd *lived* a little with.

The man who still haunted her dreams.

Dear Reader,

Thank you for picking up a copy of PREGNANT WITH THE SOLDIER'S SON.

One of the first things I learned as a writer was to 'write what you know.' Which I do find funny, because I'm not in the medical profession at all. But I know a lot of people who are, and I love research.

This book has a bit of what I know in it. The hero and heroine's son is written based on my own experience with my middle child, who in 2006 almost didn't make. I didn't have the same traumatic birth experience as Ingrid, but my son and Ingrid's son both had the same rough start in life. I remember clearly sitting in a wheelchair and the paediatric surgeon telling me, 'He's very sick. Prepare yourself.'

Spending a month in the PCCU was one of the most stressful times of my life, but it gave me new respect for the doctors and nurses who face this every single day. I'll never forget the smile on that surgeon's face a year later, when he saw my son playing with trains at his check-up. His job is so full of heartache, but his smile told me there are great rewards for practising in this field of medicine.

Now my son is a healthy, active and imaginative eight-year-old, and I look at pictures of him as a newborn and send up thanks that he's here today, scattering blocks and comic books all over my house. Except for when I step on them. Blocks hurt!

I hope you enjoy PREGNANT WITH THE SOLDIER'S SON. I love hearing from readers, so please drop by my website, www.amyruttan.com, or give me a shout on Twitter @ruttanamy.

With warmest wishes

Amy Ruttan

PREGNANT
WITH THE
SOLDIER'S SON

BY
AMY RUTTAN

MILLS
BOON

First published in Great Britain 2014
by Mills & Boon, an imprint of Harlequin (UK) Limited,
Eton House, 18-24 Paradise Road, Richmond, Surrey, TW9 1SR

© 2014 Amy Ruttan

ISBN: 978 0 263 24267 6

Harlequin (UK) Limited's policy is to use papers that are natural,
renewable and recyclable products and made from wood grown in
sustainable forests. The logging and manufacturing processes conform
to the legal environmental regulations of the country of origin.

Printed and bound in Great Britain
by CPI Antony Rowe, Chippenham, Wiltshire

Born and raised on the outskirts of Toronto, Ontario, **Amy Ruttan** fled the big city to settle down with the country boy of her dreams. When she's not furiously typing away at her computer she's mom to three wonderful children, who have given her another job as a taxi driver.

A voracious reader, she was given her first romance novel by her grandmother, who shared her penchant for a hot romance. From that moment Amy was hooked by the magical worlds, handsome heroes and sigh-worthy romances contained in the pages, and she knew what she wanted to be when she grew up.

Life got in the way, but after the birth of her second child she decided to pursue her dream of becoming a romance author.

Amy loves to hear from readers. It makes her day, in fact. You can find out more about Amy at her website: www.amyruttan.com

Recent titles by the same author:

MELTING THE ICE QUEEN'S HEART
SAFE IN HIS HANDS

**These books are also available in eBook format
from www.millsandboon.co.uk**

DEDICATION

This book is dedicated to one of my special guys, Aidan.
Buddy, I thank God every day you're here with me.
I love you with all my heart.

PROLOGUE

"WOULD YOU GET a load of *that* guy!"

"Who?" Ingrid asked as she scanned the darkened bar where she and her closest surgical best friends were celebrating her recent promotion.

"*That* guy. Down at the end," Philomena said, following her words with a whistle, a cat sound and a clawlike swish of her manicured hand. "I bet he could get me to purr all night long."

Ingrid turned in her seat to see who her friend was referring to, and when her gaze fell on the aforementioned male who made the respectable oncologist Dr. Philomena Reminsky turn feline, Ingrid almost choked on the cherry in her cosmopolitan.

Tall, muscular and clad in army fatigues, the soldier sitting at the far end of the bar seemed to have every hot-blooded female in a twenty-foot radius panting after him. His hair was buzzed short, but she could tell from the slash of his eyebrows that his hair was ebony. He would probably be even dreamier with longer locks. Still, the buzz cut suited him.

There was an aloof, brooding quality to him.

Something that told the outside world not to mess with him, yet called to the female species like a siren call.

There had to be at least ten other soldiers in the bar, but

he kept to himself, his eyes fixed on the television in the corner, oblivious to what was going on around him.

Either oblivious or unconcerned.

Ingrid loved the tall, dark and silent types. Something to do with her love of heroes like Mr. Rochester, Mr. Thornton and Mr. Darcy.

As if knowing she was assessing him, he tore his gaze from the television screen and looked at her. Even from just six feet away she could see his eyes were crystal blue. So light and intense they seemed to pull her in.

Heat bloomed in her cheeks and she turned away quickly. *What am I doing?*

This wasn't her style. She didn't flirt with strangers in a bar. She was too much of an introvert for that. The only people she could open up and talk to really were other surgeons, nurses or her patients.

Career was what Ingrid focused on. Not men.

That's why I'm still a virgin.

Well, she may still be a virgin, but at least she was finally an attending at Rapid City Health Sciences Center.

One goal accomplished.

It was why she was at this country-and-western bar with her coworkers. To celebrate her promotion. Not to flirt with men.

Why not?

Because she had no interest in a relationship. Marriage and commitment were not things she'd ever get entangled in.

"Well, it seems a lucky lady has caught Beefcake's attention," Philomena whispered in her ear.

Ingrid stole a glance out of the corner of her eye and saw that the beefcake in question was staring at her. He smiled, a crooked smile that was *so* sexy it made her heart skip a beat and her insides turn a bit gushy.

Could be the alcohol.

Ingrid glanced away again; she knew she was blushing.

"What's wrong?" Philomena asked. "He's coming over. Talk to him."

"I can't," Ingrid whispered. "What do I say?"

"Finish your drink and say hi. Maybe he'll buy you another." Philomena moved to leave, but Ingrid grabbed her arm.

"No, don't leave me. I'm not good with men."

Philomena just grinned as she detached Ingrid's clawlike grip from her forearm. "You'll be fine. Live a little."

Right. Live a little.

Except that's not how she had been raised. Her father, if he was dead, which he wasn't, would be spinning in his grave to know what she was contemplating.

He'd taught her never to take risks. To play it safe and lead a respectable and worthwhile life. Not that he thought being an orthopedic surgeon was as worthwhile as being a cardiothoracic surgeon or a neurosurgeon, but that was neither here nor there. And one risk she never wanted to take was falling in love.

Who says you have to fall in love?

Which was true.

Love at first sight was a fairy tale. One she didn't believe in. Love was for fools.

Oh, great. She was dithering. She usually dithered and stammered when she was around hot men, but that was usually out loud. Now it was happening subconsciously too.

Ingrid hurriedly gulped down her drink, the alcohol burning her throat. She tried not to choke when she sensed a large body behind her. The scent of cologne and something spicy she couldn't quite put her finger on overcame her senses.

"Is this seat taken?"

Ingrid looked up and the gorgeous, broody soldier from across the bar was standing right beside her.

Don't stammer!

"No, go ahead." Ingrid hoped there was no hitch in her voice to let him know she was a bit nervous. In fact, the whole room began to spin. She wasn't sure if it was the vodka or him.

She hoped it was him.

He sat down next to her. "Can I order you another one?"

"Sure, I'd like that." She didn't have to work in the morning, but this was also the most she'd ever drunk in one sitting.

Live a little.

Oh, God. She'd never lived a little, and somewhere, deep down inside, the part of her that her father had raised was screaming at her to run, but it was faint compared to the rest of her, which wanted to take a chance and live a little.

Damn.

Good thing her father wasn't here because he'd be reminding her how her mother had been a free spirit and that reckless behavior was the reason she'd left them.

Don't freak out and don't think about that.

"Barkeep, I'll have another beer and the lady here will have a…"

"Cosmo," Ingrid blurted out.

The bartender nodded and started to prepare their drinks.

Ingrid began to fiddle with the damp paper napkin in front of her, totally at a loss for anything to say. The opposite sex wasn't her forte. She always got so weird and awkward around them.

As was evident by the fact she could barely look him straight in the eye, and she could feel a blush over her entire body, not just her cheeks.

"I'm Clint. What's your name?"

"Philomena." Ingrid's stomach twisted for lying to him. It was obvious he would be shipping out soon and where could their relationship go? She had no time for relationships.

She didn't want a relationship.

Her stomach knotted again, and she really hoped it was guilt over lying which was getting to her and not the alcohol. With the way her usual dealings with men went, she might begin ralphing on him at any moment.

He cocked an eyebrow. "Philomena? That's an interesting name."

"I know, but I like it."

He grinned. "I like it too. It suits you."

Ingrid bit her lip. *Oh, buddy, you don't know the half of it.*

"Are you here with your comrades?" she asked, nodding toward the pool tables.

"Comrades? This isn't Russia."

Ingrid relaxed a bit at his joke. "Friends, then."

"Something like that," he said. "They dragged me out. Told me to relax a little before we ship out tomorrow night."

"Where to?"

Clint grinned and thanked the bartender as he slid their drinks in front of them. "That's classified."

"Really?"

"Well, the exact location and purpose, yes. I'm headed overseas for a year."

"A year. Well, I wish you all the best."

He chuckled. "That's it? Just 'I wish you all the best.'"

Ingrid blushed again; she could feel it right from the roots of her hair to the tips of her toes. "What else am I supposed to say to you?"

"It's not so much the saying as the action."

"Action?" Ingrid asked, confused.

"How about a kiss?"

Heat bloomed in her cheeks. "Pardon?"

"You know, for good luck before deployment."

"That is the cheesiest pick-up line I've ever heard." Ingrid laughed. "Seriously, that's…bad."

"Oh, so men try to pick you up all the time."

"Well, I have been a victim of worse attempts."

"Go on. Tell me the worst pick-up line you've ever heard."

Ingrid's gaze narrowed. "I'm not sure if I should tell you, you could use it as ammunition on some unsuspecting female."

"I cross my heart I won't." And as if to prove a point, he did just that. "Now, tell me."

"Just call me milk, I'll do your body good!"

He burst out laughing. "Okay, that's terrible."

Ingrid shrugged. "See, I told you. I hear some of the worst pick-up lines."

Clint grinned. "Well, you can't blame a guy for trying."

"Trying what?"

He leaned in closer, his blue irises rimmed with the darkest shade of blue, making the color even more mesmerizing. "For trying to steal a kiss from a beautiful, sexy woman like you."

Her breath caught in her throat. "Oh."

"I'm sorry. I couldn't resist." There was a sparkle in his eye, one of devilment.

"Hey, at least you were honest and you didn't try to pick me up with that milk line." Ingrid finished the rest of her drink. "To be honest, I thought about granting you that boon." She could almost hear her rational side screaming, while the rest of her was shouting for joy.

Now it was definitely the liquor talking.

Maybe it wasn't booze. Maybe it was all her inhibitions just letting go.

"Really?" Clint asked. "I am intrigued."

Steeling up as much courage as she could muster, she reached forward, grabbed him by the scruff of his shirt and pulled him into a kiss. What she wasn't expecting was the electricity. The heat and desire she was experiencing now. It set her reeling and her body began to melt into a warm pile of goo as the kiss deepened and turned into something raw and powerful. His tongue pushed past her lips and tangled with hers, and she heard him moan as his arms came around her body. He was so strong.

The few previous times she'd kissed men had been nice, but this was something different.

This was something dangerous.

The moment her lips touched his, it sent him off-kilter a bit.

He wasn't prepared for the shock. He wasn't ready to have his blood ignite like his veins had been drenched in gasoline.

Forward women weren't his thing. If a woman moved too fast, he pulled away.

He liked to be in control. He liked to take his time and seduce.

Sex to him was something more than just a quick roll in the hay.

So when she grabbed him and pulled him into that scorching kiss, he should've pushed her away. He should've resisted, but he couldn't make himself do it.

He was shipping out tomorrow, and he had no plans to seek out company tonight. He hadn't even planned to leave the base, until his buddies had made him.

All he wanted to do was enjoy a beer and not think about how his mother had cried last week when she'd heard about his deployment. Or how he was going to miss his niece's first birthday. Or beer, how he'd miss good old American beer, which was why he'd finally agreed to come to the bar.

He had come for beer. At least he could indulge in that one last time.

Then he'd felt someone's gaze on him and foolishly he'd looked. The sight of her had taken his breath away. Even in the dim lighting of the bar he could see her hair shone like gold.

There was an air of confidence about her but also something else, a barrier that held the world at bay. If he had more time, he very much wanted to break that wall down.

In her, Clint had seen a challenge, and before he'd been able to stop himself, he'd moved over to her. Drawn to her like a moth to a flame, and when he'd been ensnared, when he'd seen those blue-gray eyes, he'd hit on her. Something had compelled him to. Idiot that he was.

Never in a million years had he expected her to kiss him, and though he should pull away, he couldn't. He was drowning in her sweetness, her softness compelling him to claim her, to hold her in his arms and protect her forever.

He wanted her badly.

She broke the connection first, dropping her head so her forehead brushed his chin and he drank in the intoxicating scent of her hair. The scent of something clean and floral.

Feminine.

It made him want her all the more and he let his hands travel down her back, her body trembling under his touch.

"I'm sorry," she said, her voice breathless.

"There's nothing to be sorry about."

When Ingrid looked again and met his gaze there was something in his eyes, a twinkle that gave Ingrid the distinct impression that she was prey in his predatory gaze, but not in a threatening way. It was in a way that made her body burn like a white-hot flame.

Ingrid wanted him. Desired him.

Maybe he wasn't the only one giving off the vibe of

predator. She knew, without a doubt, she had a bit of the hungry eyes going on.

Live.

There had been so many times she'd come close to having sex. She had wanted to, but she'd always chickened out, the one difference now being that she'd never been so turned on before. Never, because she'd never let them through her walls. Walls that were there for a reason. This time was different. Once she crossed that threshold there was no turning back.

She wouldn't. There were no plans to marry in her future. No plans for children. Her own miserable childhood and her own parents' unhappiness had steered her off that path. She wasn't saving herself for anyone, but she didn't want to die a virgin.

When she was old and gray, she didn't want to look back and have regrets in her life. She wanted to look back and see that she'd taken a chance, that she'd lived.

Whatever the consequences were, she could own this moment. She could control this moment and never regret it. One night of passion and she wouldn't get hurt.

No promises had to be made. No fear of shattered hearts and abandonment.

Steeling her courage, she grabbed his hand. "Come on."

He cocked an eyebrow but came with her as she led him toward the exit. "Where are we going?"

"To the hotel attached to this bar." And that's where she led him. Through the double doors and into the hotel lobby.

Clint pulled her back, holding her close. "Whoa, are you sure?"

"Positive." And to drive her point home she pressed him against the wall and kissed him again, releasing every last hang-up and doubt out of her system.

She wanted him.

Badly.

His hands moved over her back until they cupped her butt, gripping her as he brought their bodies even closer together with the hard ridge of his erection against her stomach as a moan rumbled in his chest.

When they came up for air, she felt a bit dazed and out of breath.

Did she really just make out with a stranger outside a country-and-western bar?

Hell, yeah, and it was so good.

"Should I get us a room?" Her voice shook a bit.

Did I really just ask that?

"No need. I'm staying here before I head back to the base for deployment. It's my last hurrah."

"Then lead the way."

Clint led her down the hall they'd been making out in. His room was at the very end.

Her pulse thundered in her ears. Usually at this point her common sense would take over and she'd bolt, but her common sense must have scarpered because she was ready for this.

So ready.

The door opened and Clint flicked on the lights as she stepped over the threshold. When the door shut and he locked it, she pulled him back against the wall, her lips finding his.

This time there was no need to stop and talk about where they were going to go and what they were going to do.

They were alone. This was going to happen.

He hoisted her up and her legs instinctively wrapped around his waist. He walked toward the bed, carrying her, his head buried in her neck.

"You have protection?" Ingrid asked, as his lips traveled down her neck.

"Always."

"Good."

And as he pressed her down on the bed Ingrid reveled in the moment. Her moment of rebellion, of living dangerously.

It was only one stolen moment that she'd always remember.

Tomorrow he'd be gone, on his way to deployment, and she'd be an ortho attending at Rapid City Health Sciences Center.

Tonight, though, she was his.

Tonight she'd live. If but just for a moment.

CHAPTER ONE

Seven months later

"Paging Dr. Walton. Dr. Walton, please head to the emergency room, stat."

Ingrid let out a sigh, not because she'd been paged but because she was hungry. The baby was kicking furiously, and there was a great chicken-salad sandwich with a big old dill pickle just two inches away from her mouth.

She was also dead tired, but that was to be expected. She was turning into a house apparently. A giant mountain of a woman who was forced to perform surgeries like a puppet on a string—*dance, puppet, dance.*

She glanced over at Dr. Maureen Hotchkiss, who'd just wandered into the ortho lounge and who sat down like she had no bones left in her body.

"Hey, Maureen, fancy going to the E.R. for a big, fat old pregnant lady?" She tried batting her eyelashes, but that never really got her anywhere.

"Sorry," Maureen said. "I have to go check on my cast for a kid with a greenstick fracture of the upper ulna in a moment, and there's no way in heck you're big. Neither are you fat. It makes me sick."

"You're blind."

Maureen snorted. "No way. You're hormonal and delusional. Go on, I'm sure it won't be that bad. I'll watch your sandwich."

"Don't touch my sandwich or you're dead meat."

Maureen winked. "No promises."

Ingrid chuckled and with a sigh of regret set her sandwich down. She stood up with relative ease. Her pregnant belly wasn't a big issue now, but she imagined in a couple more months she wouldn't be moving through the hospital's hallways very fast.

Though she'd try her damnedest to keep up with the best of them. Right now she had control, but in a couple of months, well, she didn't like to think about it.

She stretched and then headed toward the E.R., which thankfully wasn't a long walk. When she got there, there wasn't too much activity and no one in the nearby beds looked like they needed an ortho consult.

"Who paged me?" Ingrid asked the charge nurse, Linda.

"Oh, Dr. Allen paged you. He's in room 26B."

"And it had to be me?" Ingrid gave her best pouty face. "What about Phil?"

Linda's glasses slid to the end of her nose as she looked at her. "Dr. Reminsky is on vacation and she's not an ortho attending."

Right. Oncologist and the all-inclusive Caribbean vacation that she and Philomena had been talking about taking when Ingrid was promoted. The one she had had to cancel because of her new circumstances. *Don't* live a little was Ingrid's new philosophy. She swore she'd never be so reckless again in her life.

She sighed. "Right. I'd forgotten she left this afternoon for that. Thanks, Linda."

Linda gave her a sympathetic smile and turned back to her paperwork.

She'd never met Dr. Allen before. He was new, and she hoped that he was a decent guy to work with, since she seemed to get all the trauma pages. Ingrid shuffled down the hall and knocked on the room 26B's door before opening it. "Hi, there, did someone page ortho?"

Dr. Allen had his back to her, but there was something about his stance that tugged at the corner of her mind.

It was when he turned around. "Hi, Dr. Walton…" The words died in his throat, whereas Ingrid felt like the world had dropped out from beneath her feet. She stood there stunned, like a deer trapped in a set of headlights, as she stared into those light cerulean eyes that had the darkest rims around them so they seemed to make the blue of his irises pop.

It was his eyes that had attracted her to him in the first place. The only difference now was that his dark hair had grown out from the buzz cut of all those months ago.

He'd also aged a bit, but then again war could do that to a person. Still, it was him. Clint. The soldier who had taken her virginity, the man she'd *lived* a little with.

The man who still haunted her dreams.

And for one brief flicker she could still recall the feel of his hands on her body, his lips on her skin. Those strong, large hands on her throat and in her hair as she moved on top of him, his deep voice in her ear, telling her what to do, encouraging her.

Suddenly it became very hot in the exam room and she knew her cheeks were flushing. She pulled at her collar and tried to dispel from her mind the memories of his naked body tangled with hers.

Though it was hard to do. So hard.

Dr. Allen cleared his throat. "Dr. Walton?" he finally managed to ask.

She couldn't blame him for being shocked. She'd used a fake name the first and last time they'd met.

"Yes, sorry." She dragged her gaze away from him and focused on the patient. Her cheeks were heating with a rush of blood and she knew he was still staring at her. "What seems to be the problem?" she asked, finally finding her voice.

"Dislocated shoulder. The patient, Mr. McGowan, is a bit of a golf fanatic and he insisted on having an ortho specialist reset his shoulder. I didn't know..." He trailed off and coughed. "We can get another ortho attending down here if reduction—"

"I can reset the shoulder," she snapped. It was her pregnancy messing with her job again. Once her belly had started to show, other surgeons didn't think she had it in her to reset bones and dislocated joints. Well, she could still do all of that. She'd show them. In all the hot mess her life had become, one thing she could control was her knowledge, her job. She could manipulate a joint with the best of them.

She moved toward the patient, who was on very strong analgesics and was barely looking at her. She examined the arm. "It doesn't look too bad. I think a simple reduction will be all it takes. Will you stand on the other side of him, Dr. Allen, and make sure he doesn't fidget."

"Of course, Dr. Walton."

Carefully manipulating the man's arm, she bent it, flexing it, and with the ease of having done this particular procedure many times popped the joint back into place. Even though the patient was on painkillers, he still cried out.

Ingrid grabbed a sling and secured Mr. McGowan's arm in it. "He'll need an X-ray of the arm and chest, just to make sure nothing has broken or punctured from popping it back into place." Their gazes locked again for one tense moment before she turned her back to him and started writing a script for the patient. "Have the X-rays sent up to ortho for my attention."

"Of course."

She glanced at him and smiled, but just briefly. It was

very awkward to see him and not talk about the elephant in the room. "I'll write up my discharge instructions when I have the X-rays."

Ingrid opened the door to the trauma room and got out of there as fast as she was humanly able to move.

Run. Just run.

Only she wasn't much of a runner anymore.

She needed to get away. She didn't want there to be a scene in the hallway of the E.R.

Hadn't she dealt with enough humiliation?

The questions, the looks as her belly grew?

Everyone knew she was pregnant thanks to a one-night stand. She'd just never thought that the one-night stand would show up as the new trauma attending.

The hair on the back of her neck stood on end when she heard the door she'd just shut open quickly and the heavy footsteps of a male gait close in behind her. His hand gripped her elbow and he began to steer her toward a consult room.

"We need to talk," he whispered in her ear. The mere act of his hot breath fanning against her neck made her shiver with anticipation.

"I'm actually quite busy at the moment, Dr. Allen."

"I think you can make some time for me." He escorted her into the consult room, rooms that were used to deliver bad or serious news, and shut the door, pulling the blind down.

Ingrid stood her ground. She wanted to cross her arms, but her belly was in the way. One of the downsides to being only five feet five and having a short torso, the belly took up a lot of room.

Dr. Allen blocked the doorway, and his face was just blank as he stared at her. Ingrid felt like she was in the middle of some Western movie and this was some kind of high noon showdown. She was tempted to shout out "Draw," but resisted her silliness.

"You've let your hair grow," she said, breaking the unbearable tension that had descended between them.

He cocked his head to one side. "You've changed a lot too..."

"Ingrid."

They'd used protection, but the condom, on her first time ever with a man, had broken.

Stupid Murphy and his freaking laws had been out to get her that night.

Now she was pregnant, alone and scared. Scared she couldn't give this baby all he or she needed. Terrified of not knowing what the future held.

"I thought it was Philomena?" There was a sarcastic edge to his voice.

"I lied."

"So I gathered," he said. Clint's gaze raked her body from head to toe, finally resting on her rounded belly.

Ingrid fought the urge to cover her belly but instead held her ground.

She was tired of being ashamed of her glaring mistake. She braced herself for a slew of questions.

"I'm not used to people lying to me."

Ingrid was stunned. That's what he was ticked about?

"I didn't know people are always compelled to tell you the truth. Are you telling me all your trauma patients are totally up front with you?"

"What do my patients have to do with anything?"

"I don't know, Dr. Allen. You brought it up."

"I was talking about the name, Ingrid. Why did you lie to me about your name?"

"It was a one-night stand. What does it matter?"

"It matters to me," Clint snapped.

"I wasn't looking for a relationship that night. It didn't

matter what I called myself. Now, if my misnomer is all you want to discuss, I'll be on my way. I have X-rays to examine." She turned to leave, but he grabbed her arm.

"Will you kindly let go of me?"

"We're not done here." His eyes were dark, his lips pressed together in a thin line.

Ingrid shrugged out of his grasp. "Oh, I think we are. Unless you have something else to ask me?" She waited, but he didn't say anything. "I thought not."

When she turned to leave again, he didn't grab her but stepped in front of the door.

"Is it mine?"

She wanted to slap him, but reined in her irrational hormonal-induced anger.

"What a foolish question," she said in a deadpan voice.

Clint crossed his arms. "I don't think so since you lied about your name."

"Since I lost my virginity to you that night, yes. It's yours. I can't lie or fake that."

Clint cursed under his breath and scrubbed a hand over his face. "How far along are you?"

"Seven months."

"I thought you were on birth control?"

"No, but don't you recall that night at all? I think you forget the condom you used was a bit 'faulty.'" She made quote signs with her fingers, trying to ram it in how she felt about the whole debacle. "Don't you remember what happened when you discovered that?"

Clint let out a string of curses under his breath. "Yeah, I think I mentally blocked that part out."

"I tried to as well, until the stick turned blue."

Clint dragged his hand through his hair, making it stand on end. "Why didn't you tell me?"

"Tell you what?" she asked, her frustration rising. "Oh, no, I think I might get pregnant in a month."

"About the pregnancy. You could've told me when you found out." Clint began to pace. "I had the right to know."

"Right, and how was I supposed to do that when I didn't even know your last name or what base you were stationed at? Was I supposed to contact the nearest army base and say, 'Yeah, I'd like to talk to the hot guy named Clint with the blue, blue eyes who had sex about a month ago with a short blonde woman and who is shipping out for an extensive tour of duty somewhere overseas.' I bet there's only one of you who fits that description. If I'd had a way to contact you, I would've."

Clint obviously didn't have much of a sense of humor, because he still looked a bit dazed. "Of course."

She'd been the same when that pregnancy test had come up positive. Kids had never been part of the plan, but she couldn't get rid of the child. That would have been taking the easy way out. Besides, like her father had taught her, she didn't run away from her mistakes.

Of course, now she wanted her baby more than anything, but her life, which had been so organized and efficient before, had been turned topsy-turvy. When she was home alone in her cluttered room, staring at the piles of baby stuff overtaking her clean, orderly existence, she was terrified. Motherhood was an unknown and beyond her control.

Ingrid sighed. "Look, I could've gotten rid of the baby, but I wanted it. I still want it and I plan to raise the baby on my own. I don't expect anything from you."

"Like hell." Clint's stance relaxed and his expression softened, the prominent frown lines disappearing. "I'll help the best I can. I owe you that much."

"Well, thank you, Dr. Allen."

"Clint."

She sighed. "Clint, but you really don't have to."

"I have to," he said earnestly. "It's the right thing to do."

"You're under no obligation. I'm giving you an out."

"No."

Though he was an unnecessary complication in her already chaotic life, she was secretly relieved and a little deep-down voice said that maybe she wouldn't have to do this alone.

It's the hormones. I don't need him. I don't need anyone.

She wanted to push him away, it would be easier, but Ingrid knew he had every legal right to his child. There was no way she'd be able to deny him access and, honestly, she didn't want that. She'd grown up in a broken home, her father refusing to answer any questions about her mother or even telling Ingrid how to find her.

"She left us for another man, Ingrid. She doesn't deserve you."

The tone, the hate in her father's voice still sent shivers down her spine. She had grown up without a maternal figure in her life, but since her mother had never come back or tried to make contact, Ingrid was inclined to believe her father that she had been unwanted. Denying or not telling her baby who or where their father was wasn't an option for Ingrid. This was not how she wanted to raise a family, ever.

Of course she'd never wanted a family. There was no way she'd risk her heart, only to be abandoned later on.

For most of her life, Ingrid had learned that life never ran smoothly and you had to swim to keep up.

Fate had decided to throw her a curveball in the form of defective birth-control and a hot one-night stand, and she would accept the consequences and do the best she could by her child. If the child's father wanted to be involved in the child's life, she wasn't going to deny him.

"Thank you. I appreciate that. Most men wouldn't."

Clint nodded. "I know they wouldn't, but that's not me."

"Well, I wouldn't know that. We barely know each other."

He grinned, finally relaxing. "I know, but I thought about you often when I was overseas."

"I don't know if that should flatter me or kind of freak me out."

Clint laughed. "Be flattered. You made an impression on me. I wanted to get to know you a bit better, but you left before I woke up."

Ingrid blushed. "I know. I'm sorry, but I was embarrassed. As I said, you were my first and I just couldn't face you in the morning. When I found out I was pregnant, though, I was kicking myself for not trying to get any more information from you."

"I bet." His pager buzzed and he glanced down at it. "Mr. McGowan is back from Radiology and the X-rays are ready. I'd better go."

"And I'd better check those films out so you can get him discharged." She reached into the pocket of her lab coat and handed him her business card. "Here's my info. Call me and we'll figure some stuff out."

He didn't look at the card, just stuffed it into his pocket. "I will."

"Sure." Ingrid turned and walked away. By his reaction she really doubted he would get in touch with her. Why should he? It had been a one-night stand.

He may have said that he wanted to help, but she didn't know him. She didn't trust him and she was pretty sure he didn't trust her either.

No promises had been made.

And that was fine by her.

Clint watched her walk down the hallway, her blond hair pulled back into a braided bun. From behind you couldn't even tell she was pregnant. From the back she looked like that beautiful woman in the bar who'd seduced him on his last night before he'd been shipped overseas. One he'd thought about every night when he'd been imprisoned. That stolen moment in time had been what had helped him stay sane.

He'd never, ever expected to see her again.

She's having my baby.

Only was she? She'd lied about her name. Yeah, he may have been her first, but had he been her last? What if there had been another man after him?

You saw her face when she saw you. The condom broke. It's yours.

Though he didn't want to believe he was a father, something in his gut told him that the baby was his. Though he'd get a paternity test when the baby was born to make sure.

You're a jerk.

He cursed under his breath. He used to be honorable, trusting. What the hell had happened to him?

Clint leaned against the doorjamb as the thought began to sink in. He was going to be a father. It frightened him.

How could he be a good father when he wasn't even sure where his own life was headed at the moment? When he'd come back early from his tour of duty in the Afghanistan, he'd been honorably discharged with post-traumatic stress disorder. Once he'd stabilized after a couple of months, he'd taken this job at Rapid City Health Sciences Center as a trauma surgeon.

At one time he'd loved medicine. Now not so much. Not after the horrors of war. But other than being a soldier there was nothing he was skilled at. Nothing he could do, and he needed the money if he wanted to make his dream come true, which was getting the old dilapidated cattle ranch he'd bought just before he'd left up and running again.

He'd only planned on staying until it was paid off and he had enough money to get his quota of cattle ready.

Now with this baby, that dream seemed impossible.

I can't be a father.

If the paternity test proved he was indeed the father, he was going to do the right thing by Ingrid. He was going to help her out; at least financially he wasn't going to leave her in the lurch.

He'd never do that. He had been raised properly. Clint wasn't sure about the rest, about being involved in the child's life and about being close to Ingrid again.

Emotionally he wasn't there for that.

He was numb inside.

Dead.

Just a walking ghost of himself.

Or at least he thought so.

What he hadn't expected had been the rush of intense emotions that had struck him the moment he'd seen her again. All those memories of their night together had flooded him, like he was being swept away in a strong current. Each touch, each caress was ingrained in his mind and burned in his flesh.

It was those memories of their night together that he'd clung to during endless hours of working in surgery in the middle of a war zone.

Clint closed his eyes and took some deep breaths to keep the horror of his time overseas at bay. The last thing he needed was for another flashback to overtake him.

He was new here and he didn't want to be thought of as a liability.

When his pulse returned to normal he looked up and caught a last glimpse of Ingrid at the end of the hallway before she turned down another corridor.

Clint turned back to head into his patient's room and write up a script for analgesics, but he couldn't help but look back to where she'd disappeared.

He couldn't believe that he'd ended up at the same hospital as her.

Ingrid had been his nameless salvation. He wondered

how much worse his mental state would've been had he not had that respite in the storm.

"Dr. Clint Allen to the E.R., please. Dr. Clint Allen to the E.R."

Clint shook his head, chasing away those dark thoughts. Although a child hadn't been part of his plans, especially one with a woman he barely knew, he was going to do right by Ingrid and support her financially as much as he could.

As for being an involved father?

What kind of father figure could he be to a child, as messed up as he was?

CHAPTER TWO

INGRID STRETCHED HER back. A knot was forming between her shoulder blades. It'd been a long shift, but thankfully it was almost over. She hated the night shift, especially now, but it was her turn on rotation and she had to do her duty.

To prove to the chief of surgery, Dr. Ward, and the board that she was worthy still of her promotion. Even though the first thing she'd done after said promotion had been to get pregnant.

She'd hid it for as long as she could, but when she had suffered for so long from extreme morning sickness and had needed to go on medication, she'd had to tell Dr. Ward that his new ortho attending was pregnant.

Dr. Ward hadn't been overly pleased, but he hadn't been able to fire her. That would've been a human resources nightmare, but she wasn't going to ride on that easy train. That wasn't her. So instead she worked just as hard as she had before she'd got pregnant, to prove to everyone she was in control. That she was capable of being a good surgeon still, that he and the board of directors at the hospital wouldn't regret their decision.

So even though she put on a brave face and seemed strong, she couldn't wait to go home and take a nice long, hot shower and climb into bed. Though she highly doubted sleep would come easily to her. Even feeling extremely exhausted, she knew her mind would be focused on one individual.

Dr. Clint Allen.

She hadn't seen him since near the beginning of her shift, after she'd discharged Mr. McGowan. After the discharge the E.R. had been flooded with trauma cases from a large accident on the interstate and Clint had disappeared into the thick of it.

As she had. A shattered femur had required her utmost attention and she'd spent the last several hours in surgery, trying to repair the damage from the twisted metal and carnage from the highway.

So much damage caused in a split second.

A twinge of pain knotted in her shoulder again and Ingrid winced, bracing her back. Oh, yes, she was looking forward to getting back home.

When she looked up she caught sight of a woman watching her, something familiar jogged at the corner of her mind. She took a step forward to get a better look but someone stepped between them, and when she looked again, the woman who had been watching her was gone.

Ingrid shrugged it off. It was probably just a worried loved one, wondering how a patient from the accident was doing, and she probably thought the pregnant surgeon would be easier to pin down and ask questions of than another surgeon.

She'd probably found someone closer and was talking to them.

Which was good, because Ingrid was too tired to form coherent words at the moment.

"You looked exhausted. I think you should maybe sit down or call it a night." The words were whispered in her ear as a man leaned over.

Ingrid glanced at him and saw Clint standing next to

her, his dark hair under a scrub cap as he wrote notes in a file attached to a clipboard.

"Dr. Allen," Ingrid greeted him.

"Seriously, you look tired." There was concern in those blue eyes.

"I am, but my shift isn't over for another couple of hours."

He frowned. "Do you want me to speak to the chief of surgery?"

"No, I don't want you to speak to Dr. Ward," Ingrid snapped. That was the last thing she wanted anyone to do. "I can work the last two hours of my shift. I'm not an invalid."

"I never said you were an invalid, but you're pregnant and tired."

Ingrid was going to tell him to mind his own damn business, but the moment she looked up she could see the surgical nurses, residents and whoever else was in earshot were staring at the two of them with looks of confusion.

The last thing she wanted was the rumor mill to start.

It was bad enough everyone knew that she'd got knocked up because of a one-night stand, but the last thing she wanted them to know was that Dr. Allen had been the one to do it.

She glared at those who were still brave enough to stare, one of those cold, calculating looks she was apparently so well-known for.

Most pregnant women had fits of tears. Her emotional trigger was anger and when it happened she turned into a bit of a dragon.

Ingrid needed to regain control over this situation, and fast.

"Dr. Allen, may I have a word with you? Privately." She turned on her heel and headed to an empty scrub room.

When the scrub-room door closed behind him she crossed her arms over her belly and set the gaze of fury on Clint.

He took a step back, but mirth twitched at his lips. "There's good reason why they call you Ingrid the Harridan."

"Who calls me that?"

"The interns," Clint said offhandedly. "Of course, you set bones for a living. I wouldn't expect anything less from such a young ortho attending as you. You have to be tough."

Ingrid rolled her eyes and eased her stance. "Yes, so you know why I asked you to come in here."

"This sounds like an official summons."

"It is."

Clint furrowed his brow and shook his head. "Well, I can't say that I do."

"Getting pregnant right after one accepts an attending position is really bad form. Especially when one got pregnant during a one-night stand. I don't want any special treatment, Dr. Allen. I also don't want the other staff members to know my business."

"Oh, I get it. The new trauma surgeon is showing a little bit too much interest in the ortho attending's pregnancy."

"Exactly."

"Especially since we've just 'met.'"

"You've got it."

"I'm sorry for acting unprofessionally, Dr. Walton. It won't happen again, but from one physician to another, you need your rest. The last thing you want to do is have your blood pressure climb."

"I'm well aware of that, Dr. Allen, but I have to prove to the chief that I'm worthy of the attending position I earned roughly eight months ago."

"You're quite a stubborn and determined woman, aren't you?" he asked, his eyes narrowing. "You can't control everything."

"I'll take that as a compliment." She made to push past him, but he stuck out his arm, bracing the door shut and blocking the way. "If you don't mind, Dr. Allen…"

"I do, actually. As a surgeon, yes, take my statement as a compliment. I give you props for that. But as an expectant mother, your stubbornness and ignoring your body's cues can be detrimental to your baby."

A blush crept up Ingrid's neck and blossomed into her cheeks. He was chastising her, though he had no right to since for the first seven months of this pregnancy she'd been doing this on her own, but, then, she'd said he could be involved and apparently he was taking that seriously.

Of course she noticed he hadn't said "our baby" but "your baby," and that ticked her off.

"You still don't think this baby is yours, do you?"

Clint cocked his head. "Give me one reason why I should believe you haven't had another lover since me."

Other. Lover?

Her cheeks heated with anger and embarrassment.

"Do you want a paternity test?" she finally managed to ask.

"I do."

Ingrid nodded. "You'll have one, but you were my first and only."

His eyes darkened as his gaze riveted her to the spot. There was an intensity to it that made her blood heat with longing.

She looked away and cleared her throat.

"I know how to take care of myself. I'm a physician as well. I know trauma guys and meatballers like you don't think much of orthopedic surgeons, but I know how to take care of myself."

"Look, Ingrid, I don't mean to lecture you—"

"Of course you do." Ingrid sighed and rubbed the back of her neck, which had started to ache, and her head was beginning to throb. "It was bad enough that even in this modern day and age I've had to live with the stigma of this unexpected pregnancy. Being a doctor to boot doesn't help with all the 'Didn't you use protection?' comments. I just don't want the gossipmongers at the hospital suspecting something. I don't want them to know."

"They're bound to find out soon enough. You shouldn't take all the blame for that faulty birth-control. I didn't expect the condom to break."

"Neither did I." Ingrid sighed. "It was my fault just as much as yours."

"I know." Clint smiled.

"You should've resisted me."

Clint snorted. "Right, I'm going to resist a very persistent, hot blonde from taking advantage of me before I went on deployment." The teasing stopped and he tensed. She wondered what was wrong and when she looked at him, for the first time since they'd bumped into each other again she could see the changes in him.

He'd lost weight and in the dark hair was a bit of gray. The dark circles under his eyes could be from the long shifts, but the stress lines and the way his jaw was clenched spoke of something deeper. A thin scar crossed his cheek under the stubble.

The soldier she'd had that one night-stand with was gone. This Clint was altered and she couldn't help but wonder what had been responsible for it. Then she recalled he'd been leaving for a long tour of duty, and wouldn't normally be back this quick and discharged this fast.

Something had happened.

"Is something wrong?" she asked.

Clint shook his head. "No, there's nothing wrong. Why would you ask me that?"

Ingrid shrugged. "You seemed to tense up."

"There's nothing wrong with me, Dr. Walton. I'm fine."

Only it was the way he'd said "I'm fine," as if he was forcing himself to say it, that made Ingrid think he was lying.

Well, even if he was, she didn't have time to bandy words with him any longer. She had a job to do.

"I should get back to work." Ingrid tried to sidestep him but he moved his arm from blocking her path and took a step toward her. Just that simple movement in her direction made Ingrid's heart beat just a bit faster. He tipped her chin so she was forced to look up at him.

Even though he'd changed, he was as sexy as ever. She'd forgotten just how sexy he was.

Before, when she'd thought back to that one night, she'd almost wondered if she'd over-romanticized him. Boy, had she been wrong. Even stone-cold sober, he made her feel weak at the knees.

It's the pregnancy hormones. Yes, that had to be it. Now they were making her swoon.

"Please, Clint," she whispered. "Don't."

Only he didn't move away when she asked him and she was worried he was going to kiss her, And how could she resist him?

Right now she couldn't, because right now there were so many emotions plaguing her mind she was on the verge of losing control and that was not acceptable. That was not how she had been raised.

"Stop crying. You can't control what happened. Crying is a sign of weakness. Your mother was emotional and it was because she couldn't control her emotions that she left us. Do you want to be like that?"

Ingrid shuddered and shook her father's words from her mind. "Please, Clint. Don't."

Clint backed away. "I'm just worried about you, Ingrid. I can't help it. I'm a doctor."

Ingrid smiled and sighed. "Don't worry. Just let me get along as I have been."

Clint nodded. "Fair enough, but only if you promise me that you'll take care of yourself and go home a bit early."

"Fine," Ingrid said grudgingly.

He grinned, pleased with himself. "Could Ingrid the Harridan actually be stepping down and taking another person's advice?"

"You're skating on thin ice, my friend." She chuckled and moved past him. "Watch your back, Dr. Allen."

His eyes were glittering in the dim light of the scrub room as she walked back into the hallway. Her back gave another twinge, and even though her feet were hidden in her shoes, she could feel them swelling.

The last thing she wanted to appear was weak, but going home a couple of hours early wasn't going to ruin her reputation. She pulled off her scrub cap and tossed it in a nearby laundry bag. As much as it pained her to think it, she was going to have to take it easier.

Whether she liked it or not.

Clint had made sure that Ingrid had left that evening. If she'd stayed, he would've picked her up and carried her out of the hospital, but he knew that would've just angered her even more.

Not that he cared in the slightest.

Being in the army and serving overseas in a war zone, Clint was used to doing as he pleased. Of course, then everyone would know he was the father and he wasn't sure if he was ready to take on that responsibility. He also knew she didn't want people to know. He respected and understood her reasons for keeping it quiet.

He'd spent the night in an on-call room, because he didn't fancy driving all the way back out to his ranch. Tonight, for some reason, he didn't want to be alone.

With a heavy sigh he sank down on a cot in the dark on-call room. He scrubbed his hand over his face and then lay down. Light from the streetlamps outside filtered through the half-open slats of the blind, casting long shadows across the ceiling. His eyes grew heavy and it was hard to stay awake.

Though he tried.

He tried desperately.

Sleep was when the nightmares returned. Though his body slept physically, he never felt rested when he woke up.

The room was silent for the most part. All he could hear was the hum of traffic from the I-90. It was summer and he tried to picture the cars, RVs and campers rolling across the black tarmac toward the west into Wyoming, or north toward Montana.

Then his pulse thundered in his ears as the steady ebb and flow of traffic and city noises turned to the roar of choppers and explosions.

Sweat broke across his brow. The panic was beginning to set in. There was no way he could stop it or control it. He was drowning and couldn't surface to breathe.

Then the screaming started and he could feel the muzzle of an automatic weapon at his temple.

A flash of light made him jump from the bed, ready to fight.

"Oh, I'm sorry. I didn't realize there was anyone in here."

Out of the foggy recesses of his brain, he remembered where he was. He wasn't back on the front, trying to put together pieces of soldiers like he was doing some kind of horrific and demented jigsaw puzzle. He was still a surgeon, but he was at Rapid City Health Sciences Center.

"Clint, is that you? Are you okay?"

Clint snapped his head up and saw Ingrid standing in the doorway. She was still in her scrubs. There was concern etched across her face.

"What're you doing here? You're supposed to be at

home, resting. I walked you out." He'd seen her leave. He'd made sure she'd left.

"Just because you walked me out, it doesn't mean anything. You're not my boss."

Clint tsked under his breath and closed the gap between then and scooped her up in his arms.

Ingrid screeched. "What the hell do you think you're doing?"

Clint didn't answer her. He knew exactly what he was doing as he left the on-call room and began to march down the hall toward the exit.

"Clint, are you crazy? You're half-naked," she whispered.

Damn.

Clint stopped for a moment and glanced around. A few nurses and orderlies had stopped what they were doing to stare openmouthed. Ingrid moaned and buried her face in his neck. He could see the bloom of color in her cheeks.

Well, the cat was out of the bag and word would spread through the hospital like wildfire about who the father of Dr. Walton's baby was.

CHAPTER THREE

How LONG HAD they been standing in the hallway? Correction, she wasn't standing at all. She was firmly in the arms of Clint and pressed against his bare, muscular chest. Being so close to him again made her forget for a moment that now everyone would know without a shadow of a doubt who the father of her baby was.

Why else would the hot new trauma doctor be carrying around the pregnant ortho attending he'd just met?

Oh, God. Had she just thought of him as hot again?

Yep, because right now in his arms, her stupid hormones were leaping and bounding, making her crave him like he was a chocolate sundae or a big bowl of chips. Or both mixed together.

And then she realized his chest and back were covered with scars. "Oh, my God," she whispered.

"It's okay," he murmured, understanding what she was looking at. He was obviously embarrassed by it, so Ingrid decided to change the subject.

"You're half-naked and as much as I appreciate your very ripped physique, could you please put me down and we'll find somewhere private to talk."

Clint chuckled. "You think I'm ripped?"

"Come on. I'm serious, put me down. Now." She squirmed, trying to force the issue. She needed to put some distance between them.

Clint set her down and she could hear the snickers of their audience. Ingrid kept her head down and hustled back into the on-call room, pacing until Clint followed her in and shut the door.

"So much for our secret," he said.

"You think?" Her shoulder tingled from where she'd been pressed up against his body. "What did you think you were doing?"

"No, no. I'm not the one answering questions. You need to tell me why you're back when you should be at home, resting."

"My patient developed an infection in her leg. I have to monitor it."

Clint cocked an eyebrow. "You're an orthopedic surgeon—can't the general surgeon on duty monitor your patient?"

"It's my patient."

"And that's a baby you're carrying. You should be home, getting rest."

Damn. There was no arguing that the moment he'd said "home" and "rest," a wave of exhaustion hit her. The room began to spin and she lifted her hand to her head to stave off a wave of dizziness that was threatening to overtake her.

"You need to sit down." She felt Clint's hand on her shoulder as he forced her to sit down on the cot.

"Thanks," Ingrid murmured. "I'm not this careless. I know I need to rest more."

"I know. You're a surgeon, an attending. You told me. You have drive and that's a hard thing to let go of."

Ingrid nodded. "It is."

She glanced over at Clint and couldn't help but smile. There was a flutter in her belly and it wasn't the baby kicking. It was the same feeling she'd got when she'd seen him seven months ago in that bar. Even though she'd been under the influence of Philomena's urging and a couple of cosmos, she was still able to recall the way he'd made her body hunger.

Those deep blue eyes, which could be so intense and dark with passion. Each caress from his strong hands, the way his fingers had trailed down her spine, her legs wrapped around his waist, his lips against her neck as they'd moved as one made her want it again.

Over and over.

She shook her head, trying to expel those memories from her mind, but she doubted that would ever happen. They were permanently etched in her mind. When she looked down at the baby she was carrying, she'd be forever reminded of their time together.

Now he was a colleague and she didn't want to date someone at work. She didn't want there to be any more gossip than there already was.

She wasn't going to raise a child in a loveless marriage. One that would drive him away and cause him to abandon her child, like her mother had done to her.

Other than an explosive physical connection with Clint, she didn't know him. He was a stranger.

"I'd better go." Ingrid wanted to put distance between the two of them. She ran her fingers through her hair, trying to distract him from the blush that burned her cheeks.

"That's a good idea."

Ingrid stood, but as she did so her belly tightened and a horrible cramp struck her. She cried out and doubled over as she sat back down on the mattress. It was hard to catch her breath, everything felt pressurized, like she was going to explode.

"Ingrid, are you okay?"

"Braxton…Hicks…contraction." The words came out in a staccato succession as she tried to breathe. She closed her eyes and tried to work her way through it, but she couldn't remember her breathing technique. It was too hard to focus and she was so uncomfortable.

Oh. God. If this was just a practice contraction, how was she going to get through the real thing?

It terrified her.

This was unknown.

Yes, she was a doctor and understood how the human body worked, but she was a human. A woman. One who was alone.

I don't want to be alone. And her weakness made her mad at herself.

"Just breathe." Clint's voice was calming as she worked her way through more contraction. When they had passed she glanced at up at him and noticed the dark circles under his eyes. He looked haggard. Even worse than when she'd seen him before.

"Are you okay now?" he asked, rubbing her shoulders.

"I'm good, but you're looking pretty tired yourself." She reached out and touched his face.

"Well, I was sleeping until someone came barging in and turned on the lights."

"Sorry." Ingrid stood with Clint. "I honestly didn't think anyone was in here. I'll go home. What're you doing?"

Clint pulled on his shirt. "Going home with you."

"Pardon?"

"The only way I'm going to make sure you'll stay at home is if I take you there myself."

"You don't have to do that."

Clint chuckled. "It's not a case of me being a nice guy. It's a case of having to get you there so that I know you're safely tucked into bed. Give me your keys, I'll drive."

Ingrid rolled her eyes. "And if you're going to drive me in my car, how do you plan to get back here?"

"Taxi. I think I can splurge on a cab." Clint held out his hand. "Now, hand over your keys."

"I don't think so."

"Don't make me pick you up and carry you out of here."

"You wouldn't dare!"

Clint grinned in a way that made Ingrid think she shouldn't push him. "Wouldn't I?"

She rolled her eyes and handed him her keys. He was a persistent guy, she'd give him that, but of course she wouldn't expect anything less from a trauma attending and former soldier.

This time when they walked out of the on-call room, she wasn't in his arms, but the eyes of everyone were still on them. She kept her head held high as if she had nothing to hide, but could still feel their curious gazes boring into the back of her neck.

She could only imagine what was going to be passing through the halls tomorrow. When she looked over at Clint, he seemed perturbed. This was hard on him too. It was obvious.

He didn't really want to escort her out, he probably felt obligated to.

Their walk to her car and the subsequent car ride to the town house was silent. When they pulled into the driveway she could see some lights on in the house.

Crap.

Which of her roommates were up?

All of them worked in the medical field. Theresa and Melanie were paramedics and Rachel was a general surgeon at the hospital. Also, all three of them had happened to be there the night she'd hooked up with the mysterious stranger. All of them would recognize Clint.

She pulled out her cell phone to let Clint call a taxi, but the battery wasn't charged.

Damn.

Ingrid had to let him inside to use the phone. There was

no way of getting around it; she just hoped whoever had left the lights on was not up.

Clint followed her up the few steps.

"You can see the dinosaur on top of the hill."

Ingrid glanced over her shoulder and saw the brontosaurus from Dinosaur Park. She'd never really paid much attention to it before.

"Yeah, you can."

Clint cocked an eyebrow. "You seem nervous."

"Do I?"

Clint pointed at the light shining through the kitchen window. "You got all tense and weird the moment you saw the lights were on."

"My roommates, they were with me that night."

"Ah, and they'll recognize me."

Ingrid nodded.

"Do you want me to find a pay phone?"

Yes, but that wasn't fair to him.

"No, that's stupid. Come in." She opened the door and let Clint in.

And it was. She wasn't going to make him hike at two in the morning to find a phone just to save face. Besides, Rachel was going to hear the gossip and pass it on to Melanie and Theresa.

"The phone is in the kitchen." She took off her coat and hung it on the hook by the door and then set her purse down on the table in the entranceway.

Ingrid rubbed her temples. "I think I'm getting a headache. Too much info to process."

"Talk to your obstetrician tomorrow about the headaches. It could be a sign of high blood pressure."

"Noted. Thanks for bringing me home."

"No problem."

"As I said, the phone is in the kitchen, you can call a cab from there.

"I'll get to it. Right now we have to get you to bed."

That delightful blush rose in her cheeks again. He loved that about her. The night they'd made love there had been a delightful pink blush to her face the whole time.

"P-pardon?"

"Bed. You need to get into bed and I'm going to make sure you get there."

Her eyes widened. "You're not coming upstairs."

"I am, even if I have to carry you."

Ingrid let out a disgruntled huff and he followed her up the stairs. When she opened the door to her room and flicked on the light he took a step back.

"You're a slob!" Clint chuckled under his breath. There were piles of clothes, books and papers stacked up on the desk. Her double bed wasn't made.

She was so put together and clean cut at the hospital, he liked this side of her.

The blush returned as Ingrid sat down on her mussed-up bed. "No, I'm not usually. I only have limited space for things."

"I'm taking my life in my own hands, walking into this war zone."

"Then don't. I'm in bed. You're free to go."

"No, not yet. I'm tucking you in."

"Oh, come on."

Clint crossed his arms. "I'm not leaving yet."

"Fine."

Clint navigated his way over to the bed and as she settled back against the pillows, he pulled her duvet up over her, being careful not to touch her belly. He wasn't sure if he was ready to feel the baby yet.

He didn't want to get too close. Especially if it wasn't his.

It's yours. You know it.

"There, are you happy?"

Clint smiled and turned off the light. Then he returned back to the bed and sat down on the end of it. "I'll be happy when you're asleep."

"I can't sleep with someone watching me," she murmured in the darkness."

"Do you want me to tell you a story?" He was only half teasing.

"You're a real funny guy, aren't you?" Clint heard the yawn in the darkness.

"I can be."

Ingrid yawned again. "So why aren't you sleeping?"

"Because I don't sleep at strangers' houses."

"You know that's not what I mean."

"I know." Clint let out a sigh. "I guess I'm still getting used to this new schedule since my discharge."

"What was it like?"

Clint froze. That was the last thing he wanted to think about, let alone talk about. "Terrible." He was hoping that would be enough to silence the matter, but he didn't know Ingrid.

"I gathered that."

"I don't like talking about it."

"Is that why you're not sleeping?" There was concern in her voice through the darkness.

"Partly, but right now I'm not sleeping because you're not."

It was Ingrid's turn to chuckle. "Fine."

Clint stood up and headed over to an overstuffed armchair. He removed a pile of books and sat down, kicking off his sneakers and stretching his legs out onto the bed. It wasn't long before he heard the distinct sound of Ingrid sleeping.

Her room was very cramped. He didn't like cramped spaces. This was why his own bedroom at his ranch was a loft, no walls and a very high ceiling with a skylight. He liked to be able to see the sky while he slept. When he lay his head back all he saw was ceiling. A white stuccoed ceiling that was a lot closer than he would like it to be.

As he glanced around the room he saw a change table crammed in the corner and piles of things. Ingrid's room was so small. This was no place to raise a baby.

God, he'd made a mess of her life, hadn't he? Just like his life was a mess.

Clint rubbed his eyes and tried not to stare up at the ceiling, because if he kept thinking about how confining this room was, he'd have a panic attack.

His own eyelids were getting heavy. He was absolutely exhausted and he knew that he should get up before he fell asleep, only his eyes wouldn't let him.

He was too exhausted.

There was no way he'd be getting back to the hospital.

At least this time when he slept it would be from sheer exhaustion and maybe, just maybe, it would keep the nightmares at bay.

At least he hoped so.

CHAPTER FOUR

CLINT WOKE WITH a start from the nightmare threatening to bloom. It took him a moment to get his bearings in the dark and then he remembered where he was and who he was with. It was then his fight-or-flight response kicked in. Thankfully, it was the flight aspect.

I have to get out of here.

Clint moved his feet off the bed slowly. There was a small moan from Ingrid as she stirred in her sleep, but her breathing was even, deep and steady.

It was the sound of restful slumber.

He envied her.

It'd been a long time since he'd had a full night's sleep uninterrupted by terror, by reliving his torture when he'd been captured.

Thankfully, his capture had been short-lived. Just not long enough to keep the horror of it all away.

Clint moved toward the door and looked back at Ingrid curled up on her side, one leg flung over a body pillow, her arms tucked under her head.

The face of an angel.

It had been that face that had got him through his worst moments. When he'd been working on soldiers, often without the aid of anesthetic, Clint had learned fast to drown out the sounds around him, and to do that he'd focused on Ingrid's face and their night together.

He remembered every iota of that moment.

The feel of her skin, the scent of her perfume and the moment he took her innocence from her. Her gasp of pain, the dig of her nails in his flesh and the taste of salt on his tongue when he kissed those silent tears away.

"Why didn't you tell me?"

"Do you regret being my first?" Ingrid asked.

"No, if you told me I would've eased you into it."

"I thought you might stop. Please don't regret it. I'm glad it was you."

Clint hadn't answered her, because that night he hadn't regretted it all. He'd planned, come hell or high water, upon his return from service to track Ingrid down and make her his.

Before he'd been captured, before he'd endured all the horror, he'd pictured a life between the two of them. Even when he'd been locked away in the darkness of an insurgent cell, he'd pictured that fantasy life they would share. Children, living on the ranch he'd bought before he'd left for his tour of duty. The perfection of it all.

He'd learned during his captivity that life was far from perfect and things could be broken or shattered in an instant.

That dreams were just that, intangible flights of the mind.

But when he'd got out, he'd given up on it. Not the ranch but finding Ingrid. He felt dead inside. He had nothing to give anyone.

Though as he looked at Ingrid, sleeping peacefully, the soft rise of her pregnant belly growing his child, Clint searched deep within himself for some kind of semblance of emotion, but at this moment he could only find anger, pain and fear.

Those were the kind of emotions she didn't deserve, that their child didn't deserve.

He turned and walked out of her room, silently making his way down the stairs and hoping none of her roommates were around.

He had to put distance between himself and Ingrid.

She'd planned to raise the child by herself. He'd help her financially, but he couldn't be there emotionally.

Not now.

And as he stepped outside into the chilly dawn of a new day, he swallowed down the lump in his throat and buried the emotions of disgust.

Because he was disgusted by how much of a coward he'd become.

A week.

That's how long it'd been since she'd last seen Clint. Well, that was a lie. Ingrid had caught glimpses of him, or rather the back of him. She had the distinct feeling he was avoiding her like the plague.

Ingrid also had the distinct feeling she was being watched.

Either that or she was going crazy.

All she knew was every time Clint glanced at her, he turned on his heel and walked the other way. He was definitely avoiding her.

Though she should be pleased and though his absence hadn't affected her life in any way differently, it still ticked her off.

Part of her, the part ruled by irrational hormones, felt like he should be here. Helping her. Involved.

Ingrid sighed.

She'd be glad when the pregnancy was over and she could ditch the hormones. For now she was miffed Clint was avoiding her.

It appeared that way anyway. She hadn't been around the hospital much. When she went to her OB-GYN appointment the next day, one Clint had promised to be at, her obstetrician, Dr. Douglas, had told her that her blood pressure was rising and there was a high amount of ketones in her urine.

The threat of becoming toxic was hovering on Dr. Douglas's lips.

"Take it easy, Ingrid. I know where you work and I will pull you from duty!"

Sharon's threats had been clear. She wasn't head of obstetrics at the hospital for nothing. Only Ingrid needed the extra money. When the baby was born, she only had six weeks to take off and then she'd have to head back to work. Day care, diapers and all the other essentials weren't cheap.

Why the heck am I thinking about this?

Ingrid rubbed her temples. It was just too much information. Her brain was being overloaded by the sheer magnitude of it all.

Focus.

Clint had offered help, although grudgingly, it seemed, but she'd turned him down. Which was dumb, she realized. She was going to need help, even if it was just financially, especially if she had to leave work earlier than anticipated. She just didn't like to rely on someone else.

That's not what her father had taught her. He'd taught her to be strong, independent and in charge of your own decisions and take responsibility for your own mistakes.

Her hand drifted over her belly and the baby kicked in response, as if sensing her stress level rising.

Just ask him.

Swallowing her pride, she headed toward him, praying she could sneak up on him and block his way of escape. She didn't want him rushing off again as soon as he caught sight of her. Not that she was positive that's what he was doing, but it had happened so many times that she was becoming a bit paranoid and she didn't like feeling so out of control.

Her life was about control and order.

Since Clint had come into the picture her life had been nothing but chaos. She stopped a couple of feet away from him, where he was leaning over a desk, charting, and tapped him on the back.

He turned around and Ingrid wasn't stupid—she could see the brief flicker of panic on his face before he controlled it.

"Dr. Walton, what can I do for you?"

"Can I speak with you a moment?"

Clint looked around, as if he was trying to find some excuse to take him away, but the E.R. was dead tonight. There was no escape.

Good.

"Sure." He moved toward an empty exam room. Once she was inside he shut the door. Ingrid stood in front of the door, impeding his only means of escape. "Do you really have to block the door?"

"Yes, because lately it seems like every time I approach, you turn and run the other way. Do you deny it?"

"Wow, you get right to the point, don't you?"

Ingrid shot him one of those cold stares. "Well?"

Clint cocked his eyebrow in question. "You look like a force to be reckoned with."

"Oh, I am, Dr. Allen. Never doubt that."

She wanted to add that she broke bones for a living, but kept that thought to herself.

"What can I do for you?"

The heat of a blush threatened to bloom in her cheeks, but she kept it under control as she came to the point. "Why you been avoiding me?"

Clint cleared his throat. "Why would you think that?"

"Perhaps it was something about you absconding in the middle of the night."

"Sounds a bit like a similar situation on the night we first met, doesn't it, Ingrid or Philomena?"

Ingrid bit her lip. "Fine. You got back at me."

"It had nothing to do about getting back at you," Clint snapped. "I had to return to my duties. Your shift might've been over, but mine wasn't."

"Fine. I'll concede that, but why have you been avoiding me? I'm not obtuse. I may wear different-colored socks every now again, but that's only because I can't see my feet. It doesn't mean that I can't tell when I'm being avoided."

Clint craned his neck to look at her feet, a brief smile flirting across his lips. Ingrid stifled her chuckle.

"You've got a nice mix of Halloween and Christmas going on down there."

"Shut up, don't change the topic," she snapped.

"I'm not! You're the one who mentioned socks."

Ingrid counted back from ten in her head. "You said you'd be at my next OB-GYN appointment. You were conveniently absent."

"Trauma."

He was lying. Although she couldn't really prove it. She could be neurotic. This confrontation-slash-conversation wasn't going as well as she'd hoped.

What did you expect, that he'd fall on his knees and beg forgiveness?

Although some groveling wouldn't go amiss at the moment.

"It's your mistake, Ingrid. Own it." That's what her father had said when she'd told him about the baby. She'd get no help from him and she didn't even know where her mother was.

Tears stung at her eyes. *Damn hormones.* She had to get out of there, and fast. Screw it, she didn't need to know for certain whether he'd been avoiding her or not.

"Never mind. I'm sorry for bugging you," Ingrid muttered, as she turned around and reached for the door, but as her hand touched the handle Clint's hand closed over hers, but only for a brief moment. When his hand moved off hers, she took her hand off the doorknob.

"Look, I'm sorry," he said.

Ingrid swallowed the lump in her throat and turned back. "Apology accepted."

"Is that all you wanted, to know why I wasn't at your OB-GYN appointment?"

She met his gaze. Those deep blue eyes drawing her in and making her forget all reason. "One of the things."

"What's the other thing, then?" he asked, before glancing at his watch. "I have to finish my rounds."

She wanted to ask him, but the words just wouldn't come out.

Just do it. What did she have to lose? Nothing. Clint wasn't hers. They had no relationship. All they had was one stolen night together. One that had resulted in binding them together for ever.

"Is there anything else, Ingrid? You're just standing there."

I'm standing here trying to get my courage up.

Come on. "Are you avoiding me?"

There. She'd done it.

She glanced up at him to gauge his expression, but it was unreadable. It was like a slap in the face. He didn't seem to care. He wasn't stunned, confused, hurt. He wasn't anything.

It was like he was numb.

"Apparently, this was an exercise in futility." This time she yanked the door open. "I'm sorry for taking up your time."

She walked out into the hallway, her head held high.

She was half expecting him to follow her, but he didn't and when she foolishly looked back, he had returned back to his charting. Oblivious to her and their conversation.

Well, if that's the way he wanted it, two could play at that game.

CHAPTER FIVE

INGRID AVOIDED CLINT for the next two weeks. It was a bit easier to do as she was put on a lighter duty schedule and didn't get as many trauma pages, but when she did see him in the halls she'd duck down a corridor, going out of her way to avoid him.

She was still a bit ticked at him.

As she walking down the corridor she got that distinct feeling she was being watched again, so she spun around and caught the sight of someone disappearing down a corridor, quickly. Ingrid turned to follow the person.

"There you are! Ingrid, wait up!"

Ingrid turned around and saw a very tanned Philomena striding toward her.

Crap.

She'd forgotten that Phil was due back from her vacation and that Phil had no idea Clint, the hunky soldier, was now working in the hospital.

Phil knew the hot soldier was the one who'd got her into this predicament but didn't know that Ingrid had used her name instead of her own.

Although Phil wouldn't be angry. She'd probably think the whole thing was funny, because Ingrid was generally a good girl and didn't lie.

"Phil, welcome back!" Ingrid said, trying not to sound nervous or awkward.

It didn't work.

Phil dropped her arms, which were outstretched for an embrace, and stopped. "What happened?"

"What're you talking about?"

Phil's eyes narrowed and she crossed her arms. "You're acting weird. Something happened here while I was gone."

"Nothing happened."

Phil rolled her eyes. "Puhleeze. This always happens…" She trailed off and her eyes widened.

Dread traveled down her spine and she glanced over her shoulder to see what Phil was focusing on. Though she knew.

Oh, God. She knew.

And she was right. Clint was talking to one of the charge nurses at the far end of the hall.

Ingrid sighed, closed her eyes and then grabbed Phil by the elbow, dragging her into an on-call room and locking the door.

"Oh, my goodness, Ingrid! Did you see him, did you know?"

"Of course I know. We've become…reacquainted."

"Who is he?" Phil asked, leaning against the wall. "I mean, I thought he was a soldier."

"He's the new trauma attending. I think he's actually head of trauma now."

"He's the new head of trauma?" Phil bit her lip. "How are you doing?"

"I'm fine."

Phil cocked an eyebrow. "You don't look fine. You looked stressed."

Ingrid sat down on one of the cots. "Just a bit."

Phil crossed the room and sat down next to her, putting an arm around her. "So, what's he going to do?"

"Nothing."

"Still, he should man up to his duty as a father. I mean, he's a soldier right? He should have no problem ponying up."

Ingrid chuckled. "Yeah, he was, but what does being a soldier have to do with anything?"

Phil shrugged. "I honestly don't know. Aren't they men of honor?"

Ingrid shrugged.

"So he's really not going to help you?" Phil asked, confused. "Do I have to beat him up?"

"You're really going to beat up the new trauma attending?"

Phil made a fist. "Oh, hell, yeah."

"You're an oncologist. You're about saving lives," Ingrid teased.

"Well, I can't believe he's not going to help you. Are you sure he isn't going to?"

Ingrid bit her lip. "He wants a paternity test."

"What?" Phil stood, but Ingrid dragged her down.

"No, he has every right. He doesn't know or trust me. Why should he?"

"Still, he should've recognized your name when he took the job here."

"That's the reason he doesn't trust me."

"I don't understand," Phil said.

"Well...technically he didn't know my name. The night we slept together, I used your name." Ingrid braced herself for the onslaught of fury. Instead, all she heard was laughter.

"I can't believe you did that, that's so funny."

"Funny?" Ingrid actually did a double take and shook her head.

"Ingrid, I've known you for a long time. You're one of

my closest friends, but you had a stick rammed so far up there I thought it had become fused with your spine."

"Pardon? Are you implying that I'm uptight?"

Phil walked over and sat down on the bed next to her. "Yes."

"Thanks," Ingrid said. "I love you too."

She should be mad, but she wasn't. Ingrid knew she took herself too seriously, but that was the way she'd been taught. Ingrid had grown up with this measure of expectation she had to live up to, like she had to grow up and out of this shadow her mother had cast. There were times in her life that she wanted to break free and be that reckless person her mother supposedly was.

Of course, look where that had gotten her.

Still, that night with Clint had been amazing and she didn't regret taking that chance and living, if only for one stolen moment.

"Yeah, I guess I am a bit tightly wound."

Phil chuckled and wrapped her arm around her shoulders. "What I mean is I'm glad you let loose. You just work and sleep. That's all you've ever done. I know you had a strict upbringing and it was nice to see you break out of that mold. I'm sorry you got knocked up, though. That's the last thing I would ever wish on someone."

"Thanks, I…" A pain ripped across her belly in a sharp contraction, which made her cry out and clutch her belly. She wasn't expecting it and it was definitely not a Braxton Hicks. Ingrid tried to catch a breath, but she couldn't as another contraction rolled through her. She tried to get it under control, but she couldn't. The pain was unbearable.

"Oh, God, Ingrid. Are you okay?"

"Get. Help."

Phil didn't even wait or need to hear Ingrid's plea for help as she'd jumped up and headed for the door.

The pain was making the room spin as Phil stood outside the on-call room, calling for a gurney, as Ingrid fell to her knees. She could see white shoes in her line of sight as her cheek hit the cool tiled floor before everything went black.

Clint caught sight of Ingrid, her back to him, walking down the hall. He knew since their conversation she'd been trying to avoid him, just the way he had been avoiding her.

Ingrid's suspicions were right. He had been avoiding her.

It was for the best.

Still, when she'd left the room and walked away from him two weeks ago he'd wanted to go after her and tell her why.

Only he couldn't.

Instead, he'd let her go and it was tearing him up inside. *Talk to her.*

He was going to do just that when she was greeted by another female surgeon and they disappeared together into an on-call room. He turned to walk away but then paused and glanced back at the room into which she'd disappeared.

He had to talk to her. To tell her the truth, to explain he was avoiding her because he wasn't whole any longer, because he didn't want to hurt her and the baby, because he couldn't be a good father, like his own dad was.

You're a coward.

It was a lot of excuses, but he had no choice.

He had to work. Once he'd saved enough money to fix up the ranch, he could leave medicine. Then he wouldn't have to operate anymore.

Which was something he'd never thought he would even contemplate thinking, because all he'd ever wanted to be was a surgeon and a trauma surgeon at that, but every day, every shift since his return from duty, operating was becoming harder, his flashbacks more frequent, and it was terrifying him.

The last thing he wanted to do was put a patient in danger, which was why soon he'd be able to walk away from what had been his lifelong passion.

It was just better for everyone that way.

Even if it wasn't better for him.

"I didn't raise a coward. Always be honorable."

His father's words echoed in his mind. If his father had still been alive he'd be ashamed, because Clint was the exact opposite of honorable at the moment.

And Clint's career choice had always been a point of contention between him and his father. His father had wanted him to follow in his footsteps and take over the family business, but that's not what Clint had wanted.

It had become even worse when after his intern year, he'd joined the army and gone on his first tour of duty. His father didn't want him being in the army and putting himself in danger.

Still, that's what Clint had wanted and even though they'd disagreed, his father had stood by him and they'd both agreed that as long as he did his very best and lived honorably, that was all that mattered.

Even though honorable was on his discharge papers from the army, Clint didn't feel like he deserved it. There was no honor in cowardice, and he had no doubt that if his father was still alive, he would be ashamed.

Clint cursed under his breath and turned back. He was going to talk to Ingrid; he was going to help her. He was going to make sure she and the baby were okay. That's all he had to do.

The door to the on-call room flung open and the other surgeon burst out of it, her eyes wide. "Call a code blue. I need a crash cart and gurney, stat!"

And that's when Clint saw Ingrid lying on the floor, unconscious.

God. No.

He didn't even remember how he got to her side, but he was there, barking orders as the gurney appeared. He scooped her up in his arms and set her down. The world around him was muffled, as if he had water in his ears. The only sound was the pounding of his heart, the thing driving him was adrenaline, and he was focused on her face.

"Someone page Dr. Sharon Douglas!" Ingrid's friend shouted.

They wheeled her to the nearest exam room. Clint couldn't take his eyes off her. It was like everything was moving in slow motion, but he knew that wasn't the case. Things were moving extremely fast.

CHAPTER SIX

WHEN INGRID PRIED open her eyes the sunlight burned her retinas. At least she assumed it was sunlight. Whatever it was, it was freaking bright, and she came to the conclusion that an elephant had decided to take up residence between her ears and was practicing a highly intricate tap routine.

She groaned.

"Good morning, or should I say afternoon?"

Ingrid opened her eyes and as they focused she saw Clint sitting in the chair next to her bed. His appearance was disheveled. His black hair was mussed up, a dark five o'clock shadow graced his cheeks and there were prominent dark circles under his eyes.

She tried to sit up but found she was in a hospital bed, hooked up to an IV. Then it hit her. The last thing she recalled was pain and falling to the floor.

"What happened?" she asked. The gentle rhythm of the monitor began to beep sporadically.

"Calm down," Clint said, his tone gentle. "You don't want to overexcite yourself."

Ingrid reached down. She was still pregnant, and in reassurance, the baby kicked back at her. She closed her eyes and sent up a little prayer of thanks.

"Is the baby okay?" Her voice shook as she asked the question.

"Yes, for now. It's you we're worried about."

Ingrid licked her lips. "What happened?"

"You pushed yourself too hard!"

Ingrid looked up to see her OB-GYN enter the room. At just five feet even, Dr. Sharon Douglas was a force to be reckoned with. Sharon nodded in the direction of Clint. "Dr. Allen."

"Dr. Douglas." Clint sat back in his chair.

Sharon's eyes narrowed as she looked back at Ingrid. Sharon was a friend, a comrade, but not at this moment. Ingrid suddenly felt like she'd been hauled into the principal's office. "I take it Dr. Allen is the baby's father?"

"Well, we need a paternity test," Ingrid said.

"Fine. I'll order one, when the baby is born."

"Is that all?" Ingrid asked.

"Dr. Walton, you should know better. So, what do you have to say for yourself?"

"Sorry?" Ingrid asked.

Sharon shook her head and glanced down at Ingrid's chart, making notes. "I told you to take it easy. Your blood pressure has risen to a dangerous level. You're officially off work."

"What? I still have ten weeks to work."

"Not anymore you don't." Sharon flipped the chart closed. "I want to monitor you for the next couple of days to watch for signs of preeclampsia. If all is good in a couple of days, I'll discharge you home, but it's bed rest for you until you deliver."

Sharon left the room and Ingrid let out a groan. "What am I going to do?"

"You're going to follow the doctor's orders."

Ingrid glared at Clint. "What're you doing here? I thought you were avoiding me."

Clint scrubbed his hand over his face. "It's kind of hard to avoid someone who was in need of a trauma doctor."

"Right. Well, you don't have to stay. I'm no longer your patient."

"I'm staying," he said, and it was said in such a way it made Ingrid smile. Though she'd never needed anyone in her life, never relying on anyone but herself.

It was kind of nice and that thought scared her.

"Why would you stay?"

Clint grinned and leaned back in the chair. "You're my patient, too, even if you think you aren't."

"And what about the rest of your patients?"

"I'm off duty. You can't get rid of me, Ingrid."

"I'm surprised, since you were all about avoiding me earlier."

"And you were avoiding me."

Ingrid cocked an eyebrow. "So you got the message."

"Subtlety is not your strong suit."

Ingrid sighed and leaned back against the pillows. "I can't do this. I can't do bed rest."

"You don't really have a choice."

"I'm not going to dignify that with a response." Ingrid glanced out the window, watching the snow fall softly over the city.

How was she going to be able to do this? She never sat still, unless she was studying.

She could've used the extra money and time off to take care of the baby. She'd have to find a nanny to take the baby earlier and figure out some way to juggle paying for rent, food, formula, diapers… Just the thought of it all made her head hurt.

"Where's Philomena?"

"I thought you were Philomena?" Clint asked.

"No, my friend Dr. Philomena Reminsky. She was with me before I blacked out, I guess."

"Ah, yes. Well, that explains where you got such an odd name. Does she know you committed identity theft?"

Ingrid rolled her eyes. "What a mess."

"Do you remember anything before you blacked out?" Clint asked in an odd voice that set her teeth on edge.

"No, should I be worried?"

Ingrid watched his face for a reaction, wondering what she'd said or done. Snippets of what had happened flashed through her mind but nothing concrete.

"Ingrid, come back to me."

It was Clint's voice that came through the foggy recesses of her memory. Had he been there the whole time?

"No, there's nothing to be worried about." Clint stood up. "I'm going to grab something to eat. Is there someone I can call for you? Do you have any family nearby?"

"Well, there's my father. He lives in Belle Fourche."

"Do you want me to call him?" he asked.

Ingrid snorted. "Don't bother."

Clint was taken aback by Ingrid's admission. How could her father not come? If it had been him in this bed, in a life-threatening situation, his father would've been right by his side.

"What's his number?"

"It's on my emergency contact form, but I'd really rather you not make the call."

Clint was shocked by the bitterness in her tone. It shocked him because Ingrid was so put together, so sure of herself and so controlled.

"If you don't want me to call him, is there anyone else I can call?"

"No," Ingrid sighed. "I'm sorry, it's just…he taught me to fend for myself. He won't come. I have to do this on my own."

"Dr. Douglas was clear that you need help."

Ingrid winced and her heart rate began to pick up. He needed to back off. The last thing she needed was to have her blood pressure rise or she would be at risk of becoming toxic.

It had terrified him to his very core when he'd watched them work on her, getting her preterm labor to end, bringing her blood pressure down.

And when she'd roused for a moment out of her delirium, she'd reached out and grabbed his hand.

"Help me, Clint. It hurts."

It had terrified him to see her in pain.

"What're you staring at?" Ingrid asked.

"Nothing... I'll go call your father."

Ingrid nodded and turned her head to look out the window again. She looked so small on the bed, under the blankets, hooked up to a bunch of monitors and an IV. He left the room, grabbing her chart from the door and headed over to a nearby phone to call Ingrid's father.

Perhaps Ingrid was being too hard on her father. Maybe she wasn't giving him enough credit. Though he didn't know what he was going to say to the man. *Hi, I'm the man who impregnated your daughter after a one-night stand.*

Man up.

If he didn't do anything else for Ingrid, this was the least he could do, own up to his own part in this mistake.

Clint found her father's number and punched it into the phone. It rang three times before someone picked up.

"Hello?"

"Can I speak to Mr. Walton, please?"

"Speaking."

"Mr. Walton, my name is Dr. Clint Allen and I'm calling from Rapid City Health Sciences Center—"

"Is something wrong with my daughter?" Mr. Walton cut him off, but Clint noticed there wasn't any indication of worry or concern in his voice. In fact, just within the first minute of talking to Ingrid's father, he got the sense that he was a very controlled individual. Not unlike Ingrid.

"She went into preterm labor." Clint paused, waiting for some kind of reaction from the man. If it had been any other parent, they would've been peppering him with questions right about now. "We stopped the labor, but unfortunately Ingrid can no longer work. She's on bed rest."

"For how long?"

"For the rest of her pregnancy. She's at risk of developing preeclampsia."

"I see," Mr. Walton said. "Well, thank you for letting me know."

That was it? That's all the man had to say? Ingrid had been right about her father, and if Clint had been standing in front of the man right now, he wouldn't be as cordial.

Didn't he care about his daughter?

"She needs assistance, Mr. Walton." Clint had a hard time controlling his temper. "If and when she's discharged from the hospital, she'll have to be on strict bed rest until she delivers. There's no one to help her."

"Dr. Allen." Mr. Walton's tone changed. Clint had at least evoked some kind of emotion from the man. "I appreciate you calling and giving me a status update on my daughter. I do. Lord knows, she wouldn't tell me and I wouldn't expect her to. She got into this mess and she needs to own her mistake. She's a big girl. She can take care of herself."

"No," Clint snapped. "That's the point. She can't at the moment. Ingrid needs someone to stay with her."

"What about a nurse?"

"Are you offering to pay a nurse to take care of your daughter?" Clint asked.

"No, I'm sure she could handle paying for that herself. I taught my daughter self-sufficiency, Dr. Allen. I didn't coddle my child."

The grip Clint had on the phone tightened and as he

squeezed the receiver he couldn't help but picture squeezing the neck of this arrogant, uncaring man.

"Mr. Walton, as your daughter's physician, I'm asking you to come and help your daughter."

"As I recall, Dr. Allen, my daughter's physician is Dr. Douglas. In fact, I would like to know exactly who you are and why you're calling me. Are you one of Dr. Douglas's residents, because if you are, you have a certain temerity that I'm not that fond of at the moment."

"I am not a resident."

"So you're not an OB-GYN?"

"No." The words came out through gritted teeth.

"Then I'll bid you a good day, Dr. Allen. Thank you for informing me of my daughter's status."

Before Clint could argue back or say anything further, he hung up. The buzz of the disconnected line rang in his ear.

Clint hung up and dragged his hands through his hair in frustration. Ingrid had no one. Just like he had no one.

She was utterly alone.

She doesn't have to be.

Clint closed his eyes and took a deep calming breath.

There was no other choice. He'd take care of Ingrid and make sure she stayed on bed rest. That's all he had to do. Once the baby was safely delivered, he could walk away.

Even if it was his.

He'd have to.

There wasn't any choice in the matter.

CHAPTER SEVEN

INGRID HELD UP the X-ray, squinting as she tried to examine it in the sunlight streaming into her room. It was a sunny day and there was a blanket of snow on the ground, which made the light coming into her room just a bit brighter. It was a perfect opportunity to work.

No one knew she had the X-rays. Well, the only one who knew was Rose, her intern, who had snuck her X-rays in when Ingrid had paged her. Of course, this had been after she had assured Rose that sneaking her the X-rays was okay.

She was going to get out of bed to examine them. Ingrid was perfectly confident that she could assess this case of spondyloepiphyseal dysplasia from the comfort of her own hospital bed.

They'd said bed rest, but they'd never said she couldn't work from bed.

If she had to stay in the hospital because they couldn't discharge her home, then she was darned well going to make the most out of her situation.

She hadn't been surprised that her father was indifferent and uncompassionate about her situation. Clint had seemed so angry when he'd told her that her father had refused to come out and help her, and that her father's only solution to her situation was that she hire a private nurse to take care of her.

It all came back down to her father's stance of being

self-sufficient and owning up to your own mistakes. Hadn't he pointed out to her often enough that marrying her mother and having her had been one of his own mistakes, yet he'd stood by her. Raised her, even after her mother had taken off.

Ingrid had to work. She couldn't afford the luxury of being bedridden, so she had to figure out some way to strike a happy medium, and examining X-rays from bed was that happy place.

She was keeping her baby and herself safe by staying in bed, but she was earning money by continuing to work.

In fact, she was hoping that maybe she could convince some of her staff to bring in minor splint injuries or sprains for her to examine from her bedside.

Apparently I've lost my mind.

Ingrid set the X-ray down and wondered what the heck she was doing. She'd never believed in that so-called "mommy" brain or the idea that hormones could make a woman irrational.

Now she was starting to believe it.

There was no way she could do her job from her bed, well, not the splinting or bone-setting aspects of it. It was killing her not to work.

Ingrid eyed the X-ray in her hands and held it back up to the sunlight.

"What do you think you're doing?"

Ingrid dropped the X-ray and glanced over at Clint as he walked into the room. Her breath caught in her throat because she'd never seen him without scrubs or in his white lab coat. It surprised her.

His tousled black hair was tamed, there was still a hint of a shadow on his face, but for the most part he was clean-shaven. The blue color of his shirt made his cerulean eyes pop, and with the lab coat and stethoscope slung around his neck, Ingrid almost swore for a moment she'd walked into some kind of medical soap opera.

Next thing she'd discover that she had a long-lost evil twin who'd been held captive on an island by a Russian prince or something.

I have got to turn off the television when I nap in the afternoon.

"I asked you a question." Clint snatched the X-ray from her hands. "What are these?"

"X-ray films."

"I know that, but where did you get them from?"

"I asked for them."

"You're on bed rest!"

"I know that." Ingrid snatched the films back from him. "I didn't get up and go get them, but this is a specialized patient of mine. I'm helping him with his condition. When I'm cleared again I have to do some surgeries on this young man to help straighten his limbs."

Clint grabbed the X-ray again and held it up to the light. "Ah, it's a case of SED."

"Yes, now would you kindly hand me back the films?"

Clint cocked an eyebrow and handed them back to her, but almost grudgingly. "You still shouldn't be working. You need to be getting rest."

"I have been getting rest. That's all I've been doing the last two days." She slipped the films back into their envelope. "So, why are you all dressed up?"

"I'm speaking to a new batch of trauma interns today about the joys of being a trauma surgeon."

"Fun?" Ingrid asked, though she could tell by the tone of his voice that it was anything but.

"Not really." This was said through clenched teeth and a forced smile.

Ingrid chuckled. "You don't like speaking to groups?"

"No. I don't. I like to keep to myself. I prefer quiet."

"And you became a trauma surgeon because…?"

Clint smiled, a genuine one that spread from his lips to his eyes, making them twinkle just a little bit, but it was only for a moment.

Just one flash of a moment before it disappeared.

"I don't like making speeches." He took a seat beside her bed. "In surgery, even trauma, it's quiet…" He trailed off.

"Do you want to practice your speech on me?" Ingrid couldn't believe she was suggesting it. She didn't like giving speeches and she didn't like listening to them. She'd rather be spending her time in the O.R. or setting bones. Even putting on a cast would be preferable.

God, she missed the feel of popping a joint back into place.

"You really don't want to hear me give an inspirational speech." He grinned.

"You're right. I don't. I was just trying to be helpful and kill time." Ingrid sighed.

"You're bored, aren't you?"

"How did you guess?"

Clint ran his hand through his hair, making it a bit messier. Ingrid reached out and straightened it and then she realized what she was doing and her hand froze. Clint reached up and grabbed her hand, holding it.

Warmth flooded her cheeks and they just stared at each other for what felt like an eternity.

Clint let go of her hand and cleared his throat. "I called your father again."

"You wasted your time."

"I don't think it's right, his behavior."

Ingrid shrugged, trying to act nonchalant, but it hurt. It really did hurt. Though it wasn't unexpected.

What am I going to do?

This was honestly the first time she'd asked herself this question.

Even the moment the stick had turned blue, she hadn't asked herself this question. She'd figured out what she needed to do to make this work. She'd budgeted and planned. That's how she tackled every big decision of her life.

Whatever life threw at her, she dealt with.

So why did it hurt now?

"Perhaps, but that's the way he is. So what did he say when you called again?"

Clint shook his head. "Do you really want to know?"

"No... Yes... I don't know."

"He said that you would be able to handle it on your own."

Ingrid nodded. "He's right."

Clint couldn't believe the words coming out of Ingrid's mouth. "What do you mean, he's right?"

He could tell by her expression, her pallor, that she was upset. It killed him that he'd had to tell her that her father had abandoned her.

"I mean he's right. This is my issue and I can take care of it. I've always taken care of my own scrapes."

"You call pregnancy a scrape?"

Ingrid began to rub her temples and her face began to drain of color. The reading on her blood-pressure monitor began to increase.

"Ingrid, are you okay?"

"Fine." Only the word was said through gritted teeth.

"You need to calm down."

She nodded and closed her eyes, taking deep calming breaths. Clint watched the monitors and it didn't take long before her blood pressure stabilized.

"I think I'll leave."

Ingrid turned her head. "Yeah, I should get some rest."

Clint walked over to the blind and pulled it down,

darkening the room. Ingrid's eyes were closed, her brow furrowed and her lips pressed together in a thin line. He wanted to comfort her, but he couldn't bring himself to utter any encouraging words.

Don't get attached.

That's the last thing he wanted to do.

He couldn't get attached to her.

"Try to rest."

"I'll try," she said, but her voice was tense.

Clint would tell the nurses at the charge desk to monitor her and then he'd get hold of Dr. Douglas and tell her about the spike in her blood pressure. He'd also make sure that no interns or anyone else fetched her any more X-rays. She wasn't to work. Ingrid needed her rest.

That's the least he could do. He picked up the envelope that contained the X-rays and walked out of the room, but before he had a chance to close the door Ingrid turned and looked at him.

"Picture them naked."

Clint paused. "Pardon?"

Ingrid smiled. "Whoever you're speaking to. Picture them naked and it won't seem so daunting. I do it all the time."

"Do you, now?" Clint asked, intrigued. "I have to ask, did you picture me naked the first time we met?"

"Perhaps." There was a small twinkle in her eye as she said it. "But not really. It was mostly the alcohol talking. Are you disappointed?"

"I am a bit."

She chuckled. "Maybe next time I will picture you naked, then."

Ingrid was teasing him, he knew it, and it frightened him.

"Get some rest, Dr. Walton. That's an order."

Ingrid nodded and turned back toward the window.

Clint shut the door, his pulse thundering in his ears as he thought of his upcoming speech, but that soon faded away, because now all he could think of was Ingrid picturing him naked. And then he was doing the same and that wasn't going to help anybody.

Least of all him.

Being around her was too dangerous.

CHAPTER EIGHT

INGRID HAD BEEN stuck in her bed for the last two weeks. Her blood pressure was sporadic and because she had no stable support system at home, Dr. Douglas felt the need to keep her in the hospital.

She was already beginning to have nightmares about her rising medical bills.

Insurance only paid for so much. At least here in the hospital she wasn't totally alone. At least Philomena visited her. They were playing Scrabble today, which she hated, but at least it was something to do.

"Do you want me to bring you another book? How about something spicy?" Philomena asked.

Ingrid rolled her eyes. "I've caught up on reading. I've done puzzles and crosswords. I want to work."

"That was a pathetic whine."

"I know." Ingrid whined some more. "So, has Dr. Allen been by?" There was a hint of teasing, like she knew something as she changed the topic of conversation.

Clint had been by. He visited her before and after his shifts, and they engaged in awkward conversation.

Actually, his visits were quite painful really.

Sometimes he seemed so interested and engaged in her and they chatted about cases and hospital stuff. There was no more delving into personal lives. No more talk about her father or the baby, which was good. But most of the time, he was distant and cold, and Ingrid was really getting tired of his behavior.

"Well?" Phil probed again.

"He comes by twice a day."

Phil arched her eyebrows. "And?"

"And what? He comes by twice a day."

"Oh, yes?" She grinned and turned the Scrabble board back so Ingrid could read it.

"Oh, yes, what?" Ingrid leaned over and studied Phil's word. "'YOLO?' What the heck is YOLO?"

"You only live once."

"I seem to remember you saying that to me about eight months ago and look how that turned out."

"What? You had hot sex with an army medic." Phil paused. "Please tell me it was hot, you were pretty vague about that night."

"I'm not dignifying *that* with a response." Though it had been hot. Very, very hot. "You can't play that word. It's an abbreviation or slang or whatever."

Phil snorted. "You certainly played that."

Ingrid laughed out loud as she played "hubris." As she placed the smooth tiles on the board, she felt a sharp pain. Sudden, like tearing, and she stopped to breathe through it, counting backwards until the pain dissipated.

Only just.

She had to get a grip on herself. She had to keep calm and not get her blood pressure elevated, and thinking about her one stolen night with Dr. Allen did elevate her blood pressure, though she wished it wouldn't.

Thirty-five weeks. That's all she was. Even though it would be safe to deliver should something happen, the longer she could keep the baby in there the better. Dr. Douglas had injected her with steroids that morning to further mature the baby's lungs, which wasn't a good sign.

"You okay?" Phil asked. "You went really quiet there."

With one more long, deep breath she managed to smile. "I'm fine."

Phil didn't look convinced. Ingrid was relieved when Phil's pager went off. She pulled it out and frowned.

"I've got to go." Phil stood. "Are you sure you're okay?"

"I'm fine, other than I'm bored."

Which was true. She was bored and she felt so out of touch trapped in this hospital room. She couldn't go back to her apartment because there was no one to look after her and she needed to be on bed rest.

If Dad had come... She didn't even want to think about that. There was no point.

So she was stuck in the hospital room. Wasting away. Heck, she didn't even know what YOLO was and she felt fat.

Enormous.

"You look ticked off."

Ingrid glanced up to see Clint in the doorway. Phil had gone, she hadn't even noticed her leave. She was losing her mind.

"Pardon?"

Clint moved into the room. "You were muttering to yourself."

"Is your shift over?"

"No, but I'm on a bit of a break." He came to stand beside her bed and craned his neck to stare at the board.

"YOLO?"

Ingrid chuckled. "Don't ask."

Then it happened again. The tightening, the sharp pain, like her flesh was being torn from her body. This time it was intense and it made her catch her breath.

"Ingrid?"

Only she couldn't catch her breath. It was like her lungs were about to explode. She couldn't answer him as a warm gush spread between her legs.

This can't be happening. No.

When she glanced down at the bedding it wasn't just amniotic fluid staining the sheets.

Then pain ripped through her. An intense contraction that made her cry out. She was terrified. Terrified for her baby, terrified of the pain, but mostly terrified about raising the child alone. "Oh, God. Help me!"

Clint froze as he watched Ingrid struggle. The sight of her blood made him feel nauseous, which was stupid. He was a trauma surgeon, for God's sake. He saw blood every day, but instead of moving, he was locked in place. Screams of his confinement rang through his head, screams of the men he'd been forced to patch up without anesthetic.

"Clint!"

He shook himself out of it and reached across the bed, pressing the code button. As the alarms went off, nurses and interns came rushing into the room.

"Page Dr. Douglas. Stat!" Clint shouted over the din.

He was a trauma surgeon. He was good at sewing people up, putting them back together. But she was having a child.

His child. Deny it all he wanted, he knew it was his.

This was too much for him.

"Clint." Ingrid reached out and grabbed his hand, her fingernails digging into his flesh. "I'm scared."

He wanted to tell her he was scared too, but he couldn't say anything. Everything was moving in slow motion as Dr. Douglas came into the room.

Clint couldn't hear a word she was saying as she began assessing Ingrid. All he could do was remain frozen, her hand clutching him as pain racked her body.

"Dr. Allen!"

Clint shook his head to clear the fog and looked at Dr. Douglas.

"Ingrid has a placental abruption. I need to deliver the baby."

Ingrid let out a small wail.

Clint couldn't say anything. He just nodded and watched as they rolled a gurney into the room. He stepped back, disengaging Ingrid's hand from his. He let them do their thing and move Ingrid onto the gurney as they were getting her ready to take her down to surgery.

He could walk away. No one would notice if he didn't go down to surgery.

Coward.

As they left the room, left him standing there, he had a choice to make. His gut told him to flee because if he followed Ingrid into the O.R., if he was there to witness his child's birth, he wouldn't be able to disengage himself. He'd be emotionally involved and he couldn't be emotionally involved.

He couldn't.

Clint hovered in the doorway, watching them roll Ingrid down the hall toward the elevator at the other end, and as he watched them move, he had a flashback and all he was aware of was swirling desert sand and the roar of chopper blades in his ears.

Coward.

This was bull. This wasn't him. He wasn't a coward. He was better than this.

So, instead of turning and heading back to the E.R., he ran to the elevator.

"Wait up!"

The orderlies held the elevator and he moved to Ingrid's side, taking her hand. Her eyes were wide as she squeezed his hand.

"It'll be okay. I'm here."

It was a lie. He could never be there emotionally, but he could be there for her now. He would be there for her now. It was the least he could do.

CHAPTER NINE

"How do you feel?"

Ingrid's teeth chattered. It was hard to control it. "Cold."

Even though there was a mask covering Clint's face, it was his eyes that told her he was smiling behind the mask. She may have been out of the O.R. for three weeks, but at least she wasn't totally out of touch. She knew how the O.R. worked.

"It's the spinal," Clint murmured.

"I know," Ingrid said through chattering teeth. She glanced at the surgical drape that blocked her from seeing the surgery.

"It's weird, being on this side. It's surreal not being able to see what they're doing."

Clint chuckled. "I'm sure."

"Thanks for coming."

"Of course. Where else would I be?"

There was hesitation in his voice, and deep down she knew he didn't want to be there.

So why was he?

Does it matter? He's here. She wasn't alone.

"The baby is coming, Ingrid," Dr. Douglas said over the drape.

Ingrid's body rocked from side to side. She couldn't feel anything through the numbing of the spinal anesthesia but suddenly there was a small cry, weak but a cry nonetheless, which echoed in the O.R.

"It's a boy!" Sharon announced.

A boy.

Strange emotions washed through her as she watched the nurses take her son over to the warmer. Her son. He was a preemie and the neonatologist was waiting to check her baby's Apgar score.

"Go with him," Ingrid whispered.

"No, he's fine. I'm here for you," Clint said.

"But—"

"He's fine. He's in good hands."

Ingrid nodded. "I only got the steroid shot this morning. It wouldn't have had time to work on him."

Ingrid sent up a silent prayer that her baby's lungs would be okay. She'd been in countless situations, dangerous surgeries, but she'd never felt as scared and helpless as she was feeling right now.

Was this what being a parent was like?

If so, she wasn't prepared for this.

How was she going to handle this on her own?

"How am I going to do this?" she whispered.

"A day at a time."

"I don't live a day at a time. I plan."

"You can plan all you want, Ingrid, but life doesn't always follow that plan."

He was right. She knew it better than most.

"How do you live a day at a time?"

"You just do," Clint said. "It's what I've been doing since I got home."

"Tell me about it."

Clint shook his head. "I don't want to talk about it."

"Sorry." Ingrid bit her lip and stared at the ceiling. "Can you check on the baby?"

"Sure, if you want me to."

"I do."

Ingrid watched as he got up and headed over to the warming bed. He stood back, watching as the neonatologist, Dr. Steane, worked on their son.

"You're doing good, Ingrid. Just take deep breaths," Dr. Douglas said.

Ingrid nodded her head. "Thank you, Dr. Douglas." But she didn't turn to look toward the drape. Instead, she kept her eyes on the warming bed and her son. It wasn't long before an incubator was wheeled into the room and her baby was placed inside, an Ambu bag over his mouth.

Dread knotted her stomach and her blood pressure rose, causing her vitals monitor to go off.

"Clint, what's going on?"

"Answer her, Dr. Allen," Dr. Douglas said.

Clint came over. "Dr. Steane thinks his lungs are underdeveloped. He's grunting. They're taking him to the NICU to monitor him."

Oh, God.

Helplessness was all she felt. Utter helplessness, and she didn't like it. She was a surgeon, she was in control, but right now she wasn't. She was a mother and her son needed help.

Help that she couldn't provide.

Right now, at this moment, she wished she'd majored in neonatology or pediatrics. Of course, that was foolish. She was on the table, giving birth. Even if she had the specialist knowledge, she'd be useless, but running these things through her mind kept it off everything else.

"How did he look?" she asked.

"Good," Clint said.

"Give her more information, Dr. Allen," Dr. Douglas said. "Good won't cut it. She's hormonal."

"It's okay, Sharon!" Ingrid smiled up at Clint. "Do you have a preference for a name?"

Clint cocked his head to one side. "No. Why don't you name him? Anything you want."

"Anything I want? So I could name him Franklin or Hawk or—"

"Okay, not anything. Seriously, Hawk?"

Ingrid laughed. "It's hard to laugh when your body is frozen."

Clint chuckled. "I bet."

"So no Hawk."

"No Hawk. I veto Hawk and Franklin. It's like you're naming him after a turtle or something."

"I wasn't seriously considering Franklin. What about Jase?"

"I can live with Jase."

She smiled. It was the first time he'd agreed with her on something about the baby.

"Have you decided on a name?" Dr. Douglas asked.

"Yes, Jase." Ingrid nodded, because that's all she could do, strapped to the table. "Jase."

"I like that name. Good choice, Mom and Dad. I've almost finished my suturing."

"Dad?" There was tension in Clint's voice. "I don't think I'm ready to be called that."

"But you are," Ingrid said.

Clint sighed. "Not yet. The test."

Ingrid's eyes stung with tears, which were threatening to spill, and she tried to hide her disappointment. "Right. Of course."

Ingrid just shook her head and stared back up at the ceiling as Dr. Douglas finished her suturing. A C-section wasn't something she had planned on. A C-section would take a long time to recover from and she'd need help.

What the heck was she going to do?

CHAPTER TEN

THE PATERNITY TEST came back positive.

He was Jase's father.

Honestly, he had known that the moment he'd seen him.

He should've canceled the test and saved himself the expense, but he was an idiot.

Still, he wasn't sure if he was ready to be a father. So he kept his distance still because he refused to hurt Ingrid and Jase. He didn't want to saddle them with a damaged army medic.

They both deserved so much more.

More than he had to offer at the moment.

Clint watched as Ingrid moved around the room, packing her bag. She had been discharged, though Jase had not, and she was going home alone.

Unless you do something about it.

But if he asked her to move in with him, he was getting totally involved.

She winced as she reached for something.

He couldn't leave her to her own devices.

Not when their son was in the NICU still. Not when she needed help to heal.

There was no one to help you heal.

Clint cursed under his breath and dragged his hands through his hair. He should turn around and walk away, but he'd been telling himself that since she'd walked into the trauma room pregnant and he'd realized he was the father.

Only he couldn't turn away.

He was no good for her. He was damaged goods and Ingrid deserved much more.

"Oh, hell."

He pushed open the door to her room. She looked up and cocked her eyebrows in question.

"How are you getting home, Ingrid?"

"A taxi."

"Good. I'm glad you're not driving."

Ingrid shrugged her shoulders. "I know the routine. No driving for six weeks, no heavy lifting, no…" And she blushed then cleared her throat. "Sex."

Clint cocked an eyebrow. "And that's important to you?"

Ingrid frowned. "No. I'm just regurgitating my post-op notes." It took a moment for her cheeks to turn back to their normal color, though he liked being able to affect her like that.

"Who's going to take care of you?"

"Me."

"Then how are you going to get back and forth to the hospital to see Jase?"

Ingrid licked her lips. "Taxis, I guess, that is when I can't get a ride with my roommates."

"How do your roommates feel about having a premature baby living with them? That is, of course, when Jase is discharged."

"Well, that won't be for a while. You heard Dr. Steane's diagnosis. He needs time on the ventilator to allow his lungs to develop."

Clint swallowed the lump in his throat. It scared him, but he had to keep it together. He couldn't let his emotions get hold of him. "I was there."

"So I have some time." Ingrid winced again and pressed

her hand against her abdomen, before slowly sitting down in a chair. Clint watched her, taking deep breaths. Her usually neat blonde hair was frizzy and unkempt. Her clothing was bagging, her face pale and there were dark circles under her eyes.

And she was still beautiful.

He still desired her and that thought terrified him to his very core.

Walk away. Just turn around and walk away.

"You had a rough experience. You lost a lot of blood and spent a week in the hospital after giving birth. You're stressed and—"

"What's your point, Dr. Allen?" Ingrid asked, her voice tired.

"Move in with me."

Ingrid had to shake her head. Had she heard that correctly? "Move in with you?"

"I want to take care of you. I can take you back and forth to see Jase. You wouldn't be alone."

"I'm not alone."

Only she was. She was alone.

Her roommates all had crazy schedules. A baby crying at all different hours of the day and night would disrupt the entire household.

And the room she lived in was tiny, messy, chaotic, and it stressed her out.

The crib she had for Jase was crammed in the corner of the room. All she had was a narrow path from the crib to her bed and the top of her dresser had to be transformed into a change station.

She'd thought she was prepared. She'd thought she was in control.

Then again, she'd thought she'd had more time before

Jase made his entrance into the world. His birth wasn't supposed to be like that.

It was hard to let go of things she'd planned and worked out in her head. But as she glanced down at her baggy shirt and pants she realized she'd already lost control. She just didn't know when it had happened.

"I am alone," she finally admitted with a ragged breath. "You're right. I'm alone."

"Move in with me. I have more than enough room. I live on a ranch, for heaven's sake."

"Aren't you moving a bit fast?"

He grinned. "Right, because we've taken it slowly up to this point."

She laughed. "Good point."

"Move in with me."

"Do you think that's wise? We barely know each other."

Clint crossed his arms. "We've known each other for, what, a month now. Just over a month. We have a son together. I was there when he was born and we work together. I think it's safe if you move in with me."

He scrubbed his hand over his face and took a seat on the end of the bed, facing her. "You've been through the wringer, but you're alone. You'd have your own room and you'd have your own bathroom."

"Wow, that sounds like some kind of ranch house."

Clint smiled. "Well, it's not quite finished yet. The interior is almost complete. The outside is a bit dilapidated."

"I thought you didn't want anything to do with Jase."

"What gave you that idea?"

"Well, first you didn't believe he was yours, even though he is." Ingrid shrugged. "You're so cool and distant when it comes to him. The nurses tell me you don't go and see him."

"I've been busy. Look, I can take care of you. You can stay with me until you get back on your feet. It doesn't have to be a permanent thing."

It was the way he'd said *"It doesn't have to be a permanent thing."*

What did that mean? Did that mean that it could be a permanent thing? She didn't want permanence. No, she was terrified by the idea.

"What do you say, Ingrid? Are you going to let me take you home?"

"Okay, because it's just for now." It was the right choice. This choice would benefit Jase and not turn her friends into her enemies because they couldn't stand the sound of her baby crying at two in the morning. At least until she got her feet back under her. Then she could move out on her own. This would be better for Jase but not for her.

She was going to be trapped under the same roof as Clint.

The only man who had ever convinced her to throw caution to the wind and have a one-night stand. He was the only man she'd ever been with. The only one she thought about still.

Oh, God. How am I going to do this?

"Ingrid, you're blanking out."

Ingrid shook her head. "Sorry, yes. I'll move in with you, for now." She emphasized that part.

"Good, because that's what I told Dr. Douglas when she signed off on your discharge." He smiled smugly.

"You told Sharon that, without asking me?" Ingrid cursed under her breath. "Assume much?"

Clint shrugged. "Well, I wasn't sure for a while that I was going to ask you to move in with me."

"Really?"

Clint sighed. "Look, I haven't been sure about a lot of things, especially since my discharge from the army. My plan is to eventually leave surgery and just live off the land on my ranch. I want solitude and quiet."

"You're trauma."

"We've had this conversation." Clint stood up and grabbed her suitcase. "Come on, we're going, but you just wait there until I get you a wheelchair."

"I don't need a wheelchair."

Clint glared at her. "Hospital procedure. You'd think after all that other information you'd remember that it's hospital policy that surgical patients be taken out of the hospital by wheelchair."

Ingrid sighed. "Fine. I'll wait here for the wheelchair."

Clint nodded. "Not that you have a choice. Remember, no lifting, no driving." He turned, then snapped his fingers. "Oh, and no sex."

There was a glint to his eye when he said it, one that made Ingrid blush.

"Would you get my wheelchair before I change my mind?"

He nodded and left.

Ingrid leaned back in the chair. What was she doing?

The only thing she could think of was that she was trying to give Jase a better life.

She was trying to give him access to both his parents, because the last thing she wanted to do was have Jase grow up without knowing his father. She didn't want her son to grow up the way she had.

CHAPTER ELEVEN

THERE WAS LIGHT fluffy snow in the air as Clint drove Ingrid along I-90, northwest toward Blackhawk, and because of the snow it was a bit slow going, but Ingrid didn't mind in the least. She loved the snow and she loved it falling from the sky in large, fluffy flakes.

"I didn't realize you lived so far out of town."

"It's not too far," Clint replied as he took the next exit. "On a good day it's about a twenty-minute drive to the hospital. I like the solitude and in the summer the foothills are marvelous."

"I love the badlands," Ingrid sighed.

Clint smiled. "So do I."

"It's why I chose to do my internship and fellowship in Rapid City. I got offers from Mayo and some west coast hospitals."

"Really? An offer from Mayo. What did your father think about it?"

"About what?"

"About you turning down the offer from Mayo."

Ingrid turned and looked back through the window at the falling snow. Her father had almost gone through the roof when she'd told him she'd accepted a residency at Rapid City Health Sciences Center instead of Mayo.

There had been many arguments about it.

Threat of him disowning her, and then he'd laid on the

guilt trip, but Ingrid was just as stubborn as he was and had held firm.

It's why she lived with a bunch of roommates instead of staying at her father's house in Belle Fourche. She wasn't welcome to stay under his roof because she didn't do what he wanted.

It's why her mother had left. At least, that's what he'd said.

She understood that. What she didn't understand was why her mother had left her behind. That was hard to forgive.

It was also why Ingrid didn't want to get involved with anyone. She didn't want any man to have any say over her life, but she also wasn't going to cut Jase off from his father. No, she wasn't going to make that mistake.

"You've gone awfully quiet."

Ingrid snorted. "What do you think? You spoke to him. Twice. Besides, why do I have to share everything? You've hardly opened up to me."

She glanced over at Clint and he was frowning as he turned down a side road. "What do you mean?"

"Any time I ask you a personal question you clam up."

"You've only ever asked me about my time overseas, which I won't talk about. You know that."

Ingrid nodded. "Okay, well, why don't you tell me about your family?"

"Mother, father, sister and a brother." Clint flicked on his blinker. "Oh, and a niece and nephew."

"How very concise of you."

"You haven't told me much about your family either. I've talked to your dad, but is there anyone else?"

"My mother left when I was young. I don't remember her. Is that what you wanted to know?"

"I'm sorry." Clint glanced at her.

Ingrid shrugged. "It is what it is. So, what about your

mother, father, sister and brother? Tell me about them. They're Jase's family now."

"I guess they are." There was a brief smile on Clint's face and then it disappeared. "I don't want to talk about them."

"Why? Did they disown you?"

"No, my father is dead and the rest of my family...the rest of them don't even know I'm back from my tour of duty."

"What?" Ingrid was shocked. "Why—?"

"Here we are," Clint interrupted.

Ingrid tore her gaze from him as they pulled up a long drive to a house that did look a bit dilapidated on the outside. He parked and exited the car, grabbing her bag from the back before coming to her side of the car and opening her door to help her out.

"It looks...nice."

Clint grinned. "I warned you that the outside wasn't much to look at."

"And you're so confident that the inside is better."

"Very confident. I'm a surgeon and I'm good with my hands." He winked.

He guided Ingrid up the snowy path and then unlocked the front door. "Welcome home."

Ingrid stepped inside and she was surprised.

Inside it was very rustic, with exposed beams, stone on the fireplace at the far end of the living room, and skylights in the cathedral ceiling meant that the house was flooded with natural light.

The decor was leather and minimalistic with dark plaids. Very manly, but Ingrid liked that look. It's what she'd grown up with in her father's house.

The only difference was that her father's taste was a bit more classical.

She preferred this.

Really preferred this.

"What do you think?" Clint asked. There was a twinkle of excitement in his eyes. Pride of ownership. The last time she'd seen this look had been nine months ago, the night they'd conceived Jase.

"It's great. It's beautiful."

"Your room is over here, on the other side of the kitchen."

Clint led her through the massive kitchen, which was just as impressive as the rest of the house.

"Where did you find time to do all of this?"

Clint shrugged. "I'm not always at the hospital."

"Could've fooled me."

He grinned and opened up the room. "Here's the guest room. There's an en suite."

Ingrid wandered into the room. It was larger than her room back at the house. It wasn't as rustic as the rest of the house, but it was a nice room with large bay windows. She held her stomach as her incision site stung.

She sat down slowly on the bed and watched the snow-flakes fall outside her window. She was exhausted and she was missing Jase. She wanted to be at the hospital, where she had access to her son.

Then it hit her. More pain but not physical. It was emotional, and she didn't want to cry in front of Clint so she held it in, even though it hurt.

"Are you going to be okay?" Clint asked, as he set her suitcase on the dresser.

No.

"Yeah, I'm just tired."

He nodded. "You look tired. Why don't you rest and once you've napped we can head back to the hospital and you can visit Jase?"

Ingrid was struck by the *you,* not we, but she was too tired to analyze it. "That's a good idea."

She really did need a nap. She hadn't been sleeping well.

Clint left the room, shutting the door gently. Ingrid curled up on the bed, on top of the comforter. She lay on her back, because for so many months she hadn't been able to because Jase would press on her uncomfortably.

She turned her head to the window so she could see the snow falling outside and watched the snowflakes until she couldn't see them anymore.

The buzzing sound of an electric saw or some other kind of power tool woke her up. It felt like her head was full of cotton and when her eyes adjusted she realized it was dark outside. The only light shining through her window was from an unknown outside light.

She got up slowly and made her way to the window to peer outside. It was still snowing, but the fat, fluffy flakes were thicker, denser, and there was a lot of build-up on the ground.

The buzzing sound started again and then it was followed by a crash and a bang. She ran her fingers through her hair and headed out of her room.

She was not prepared for what she saw when she walked into the kitchen. Clint, shirtless in tight jeans, sweat pouring down his back as he hammered and sawed. It looked like he was putting up a room off the large living room. A room that was close to hers.

When he'd said he did all the work himself, she almost hadn't believed it. Surgeons were good with their hands, but they dealt with meticulous sutures, tissue, organs. Things that required a gentle touch.

Hammering, sawing and building walls was tough work and could injure the hands.

It was kind of hot to watch, though.

What are you doing? No sex for six weeks.

It's not like she was missing anything. The one and only time she'd done it had been with Clint. She'd only had it once. Okay, twice that night and, yes, it had been good. At least she thought so, but then again she had nothing to compare it with.

Ingrid rubbed her temple. When had she suddenly become so obsessed with sex?

Hormones. It had to be the hormones. She'd blame as much as she could on hormones.

The buzzing stopped and Clint stretched. She stood transfixed, watching his muscles roll and move under his skin. She'd forgotten how built he was.

Get a grip. Say something so he doesn't think you're ogling him.

She looked down at the ceramic tiled floor, tiles he'd probably laid himself, and cleared her throat before she looked up again.

"Ingrid? Did I...did I wake you up?"

"Yeah. What time is it?"

Clint set down whatever power tool he was using and glanced at the wall. "After midnight."

"What happened to going back to the hospital?"

"The roads closed." Clint wandered over to a cupboard and pulled out a glass tumbler. He filled it full of water at the fridge. "I thought it was best to let you sleep. You were snoring pretty loudly when I checked on you."

"I don't snore!" Ingrid said haughtily.

Clint downed the water. "You do. Loudly."

Ingrid rolled her eyes. "Well, at least I don't operate heavy machinery at midnight to wake up my guests."

"My apologies. I'm so used to being on my own. I don't sleep well, so I work on the house."

Ingrid glanced around the kitchen. "How long have you had this place?"

"Two months."

"You don't get a lot of sleep, then."

Clint shrugged. "I sleep at the hospital in the on-call rooms, that is when I'm not carrying pregnant ladies out."

Ingrid blushed. "Sorry about that. I know…I know you didn't want to be involved with my situation."

"What's done is done. We don't need to talk about the past. Is there anything I can get you?"

"Maybe something to eat. I haven't eaten since I was discharged."

He smiled. "No problem. Just let me put on some clothes."

He turned back into the living room and Ingrid watched him head up the stairs, stairs she hadn't notice when she'd first arrived.

It was only a couple of minutes and he was back in a fresh set of clothes and standing in front of her. "What do you want?"

"What do you have?"

"How do you feel about scrambled eggs?" Clint asked as he opened the fridge.

"I would love scrambled eggs."

"Take a seat over there." Clint nodded toward the oak table. "Sorry, I don't have any bread"

"It's okay. Protein is good for healing."

Clint cocked an eyebrow as he pulled down a frying pan. "Is it?"

"Builds muscle."

"True." He went about cracking the eggs into the pan. "Sorry I don't have much in the house. I'll have to rectify that now I have someone living with me."

Living with him? It made her panic. She wasn't living with him.

"Don't you mean staying with you?"

Clint paused as he turned on the gas burner. "Right."

The eggs smelled awesome. She couldn't remember the last time she'd had scrambled eggs. Most of the time when she was working, she would grab sandwiches or salads or some other low-calorie microwaveable meal.

Sometimes dinner consisted of cereal.

"Voilà." Clint slid the eggs onto a plate and set it in front of her, before taking a seat across from her. "Let me know what you think."

She picked up her fork and took a bite. "Very good."

"I pride myself on my cooking. I could make something out of nothing, especially when I was overseas."

Ingrid was surprised that he'd started talking about his time overseas. Any time he came close to speaking about it, he became closed off and distant.

"I thought you said you were a medic. I didn't think you were a cook."

"Sometimes, in the thick of it, we didn't have access to a cook and you just had to make do. Most other medical professionals in the MASH unit were terrible cooks. Absolutely horrible. I couldn't stand eating their swill, so I learned to cook."

"You're a true Renaissance man, Clint."

"How about some OJ?"

"That would be great."

Clint got up and pulled a carton of orange juice out of the fridge, pouring her a glass and then pouring himself one before returning back to the table. Ingrid finished the eggs and gladly took the glass of OJ.

"So you know how to renovate, you know how to perform surgery and you can cook. I know how you learned to cook and you got your medical training at school, so tell me where you learned how to construct things."

Clint's gaze narrowed and he leaned back in his chair. "Why this curiosity about my building skills?"

"What are you building over there?" Ingrid nodded to the recent construction. "You're putting up walls."

She wanted to ask about the emotional walls he was putting up, but it wasn't her place. So instead she would just ask about the actual physical walls that were encroaching on his open concept living room and kitchen feng shui.

"The baby's room."

"I thought you had a room for Jase? I don't want you to go to any trouble—"

Clint held up a hand. "It's no trouble. He needs his own room. Look, when I had to get you clothes to come home in, I saw the cramped set-up you had going on in that room. You need your own space. Every mother needs their own space—at least, that's what my mother said."

Ingrid grinned. "Must be nice."

"What?"

"To have a mother. I wouldn't..." She trailed off and dropped her head into her hands, trying not to cry, because suddenly thinking about how she'd grown up without a maternal presence hit close to home. How could she be a mother when she didn't even remember hers?

She didn't know how to be a mother.

Clint at least had a mother, even though he hadn't told her he was back. That irked her. Why hadn't he told his family he was back? He had a family, obviously a loving family. She only had a father, who didn't give two figs about her or his grandson.

But Clint had people who loved him and he hadn't even told them he was back. She swallowed the lump in her throat, keeping the tears in check.

Ingrid cleared her throat again and pushed her plate away. "So, who taught you carpentry?"

"My father. He owned a construction company. He always wanted me to join him, but medicine was my passion, as was the... Well, it doesn't matter anymore."

Ingrid nodded. "I think I'll go to bed. Maybe after a shower, and then I'll go to bed properly, instead of lying on top of the covers."

"I'll call it a night too. The roads should be cleared to-morrow. I'm on an eight-hour rotation, but you can spend the day with Jase."

Ingrid nodded again. "That sounds good."

And it did.

She missed her baby. She wanted to see him, even if she could only touch him through the incubator.

"Good night, Clint, and thanks for the scrambled eggs."

She got up and moved toward her bedroom.

"There are towels in the armoire," Clint called after her.

"Thank you." Ingrid closed the door to her bedroom.

Shower and sleep. That's what she needed.

Of course, she needed more. An emotional connection, a human touch. She needed to be held, to be told it was all right.

She'd never had that before. Why should she expect it now?

She shouldn't, but she wanted it all just the same.

CHAPTER TWELVE

"WE NEED TO get this man up to an O.R., stat!" Clint held his hands on the man's chest, trying to keep the blood from gushing out of the gunshot wound in his chest. He hated guns. He hated the destruction they caused.

The doors opened and his interns pushed the gurney toward the O.R. while he barked orders, and as they raced down the hall, flashes of his time in the insurgent compound flashed around him.

Familiar faces of his captors began to appear in the crowds as he moved down the halls.

Focus.

Clint shook his head to clear the thoughts. He couldn't let them jangle his mind right now. He couldn't lose control. The life of the man beneath him depended on him keeping it together.

When they were in the O.R., he leapt off his patient and had one of his residents take over as he scrubbed in.

He pressed the bar and let the water run over his hands, scrubbing them over and over with soap.

"Dr. Allen?"

Clint turned to see Ingrid's replacement standing there with an X-ray. "Yes, Dr. Misasi."

"His X-rays show that he has fractured ribs."

Dammit.

Clint took the X-ray and held it up to the light. "It's not too bad. We can still go in. Will you assist me, Dr. Misasi?"

Dr. Misasi nodded his head. "Of course."

"Good. Scrub in. We have to move fast. The patient is losing a lot of blood."

"Right away."

"Amputate his arm. Do it now!"

Clint froze as that voice from his past infiltrated his brain.

"Give me some morphine or something!" Clint demanded from the insurgent.

"No. You will do the amputation now or I will lash you again. Do it. Do it now."

Clint glanced at the young boy, shivering.

"I'm sorry. So sorry."

"Dr. Allen?"

Clint jumped and gripped the sink. He was still in the scrub room. The clean, antiseptic scrub room, and beyond him was his patient with a GSW, one who was sedated and would receive the correct care.

This patient wouldn't feel him cracking his chest.

This patient wouldn't scream.

The screams echoed between his ears.

Shake it off.

"Dr. Allen?" Dr. Misasi asked. "Are you okay?"

"Perfectly." He took a deep breath. "Let's go."

He turned back to the sink and began to scrub it all away. He had to keep the flashes of his capture away.

Right now he had a job to do.

When he was done, he headed into the O.R. where his scrub nurse gowned him and held out gloves which he slipped his hands into.

"He's ready for you, Dr. Allen," Nurse Warren said.

Clint headed over to his patient, but not before he

glanced up into the gallery and saw Ingrid sitting there. She was the only one in the gallery, watching.

It gave him a thrill that she was here watching him.

Keep it together.

"Ten blade."

I miss surgery.

Ingrid watched longingly through the gallery window as Clint operated on a police officer who had been shot in the line of duty.

She'd spent the morning with Jase. Not that they had much interaction with him being on a ventilator, but he was doing good. His lungs were developing and he may be able to come off it soon.

Which meant it wouldn't take long before he'd be home. Which was great but it also scared her. Another unknown. Still she longed to hold him. Though she missed work, too.

When she was in the O.R. or when she was setting bones, she could clear her mind. If she was just a general surgeon then she could get back to work, even on light duty, but she wasn't a general surgeon. She was an ortho surgeon.

An ortho attending.

And an ortho attending needed to have the full use of her abdominal muscles. Setting bones required a lot of muscle. Bones were hard, they took a beating.

Everything about the specialty required strength and guts.

It's what she loved about it.

Her father had wanted her to be a cardiothoracic surgeon. Something that required a gentle touch. Cardiothoracic surgeons got paid more.

Ortho was dirty and gritty and not suitable for a lady, but when she'd been ten she'd broken her arm and this amazing female ortho surgeon had set her bone and wrapped her cast in pink gauze and then signed it.

Her father had thrown away that cast, but Ingrid had never forgotten the surgeon. Never forgotten that moment. It's when she'd decided that's what she wanted to do.

There was something poetic and beautiful about resetting bones.

When you were a surgeon, when you were passionate about what you did, there was nothing that could stop you.

Clint could've been a carpenter, but he'd chosen surgery instead of his father's business. He'd chosen the army to better his skills.

So why did he want to give it up?

Clint was a mystery.

He had pretty thick emotional walls, but so did she, and she wasn't ready to bring them down yet.

The walls were her protection. She needed them.

Her incision twinged and she stood up. It was hard to stand without hunching over, but hunching would be bad for her abdominal muscles and she needed her muscles.

In six weeks, she'd be clear for surgery.

She didn't know what she was going to do with Jase. That was still a worry.

Ingrid closed her eyes and rubbed her neck.

How she envied Clint down there. He was right. There was a quiet solitude to working in the O.R. It was somewhere to collect your thoughts.

It was why she'd come to the gallery to watch him. She was hoping some of that peacefulness would permeate through the walls and that she could get a clear thought in her head, but it wasn't working.

She glanced back down at him. His hands in the man's chest, saving his life. Her replacement, Dr. Misasi, working beside him.

It could've been her if she hadn't been so stupid that

night, but then again if she hadn't thrown caution to the wind she wouldn't have met Clint and she wouldn't have Jase.

So she didn't regret it.

She may not feel like much of a mother or a surgeon or even a desirable woman at the moment, but she didn't regret anything.

Ingrid turned to leave, but then stopped when she saw there was a commotion down below. Clint was frozen and she could tell from the monitors that the patient's vitals were acidotic.

She pressed her hands against the windows and watched.

What's going on?

It felt like an eternity, watching as Clint just stood still, his hands in the man's chest. Only it was only for a moment and then he shook his head and continued working. The patient stabilized.

What had just happened?

And then it hit her and she wondered if Clint had been discharged from the army because something had happened over there. Something terrible.

And if that was the case, should he really be operating?

Only she wasn't the chief. She knew nothing about Clint and that was not her call.

Ingrid sat back down in the chair.

Whatever it was, she was going to help him through it.

CHAPTER THIRTEEN

SHE'S SINGING TO **him.**

Clint froze before he entered the NICU. He'd finished his shift and come to take Ingrid back home, and when he'd heard she was in the NICU, it had been hard to make himself come here. He hadn't been since the day Jase was born. He was a coward when it came to his son.

The emotions Jase stirred in him terrified him.

It was the flood, the rush he felt. He'd been numb for so long that he hadn't been expecting it.

First, seeing Ingrid again when he'd never thought he would, then Jase's birth, and now she was sitting beside Jase's incubator and singing to him.

It nearly broke him.

He'd seen her in the gallery when he'd been doing the surgery. Had she noticed when he'd hesitated?

His scrub nurse had. His interns had.

"Dr. Allen?"

"Dr. Allen, the patient is becoming acidotic."

"Dr. Allen!"

He'd hoped that the flashbacks would've stayed in the scrub room. When he was operating, the flashbacks usually stopped.

Of course, the flashbacks had only started out in his dreams. Which was why he'd managed to do so much work on the inside of his home.

Now they were intruding on his conscious time and he wasn't sure what he was going to do. He needed more time. He couldn't give up his job as a surgeon. Not yet.

Soon his ranch would be paid off.

Of course, now he had Jase.

He needed to keep his job as a surgeon and he couldn't let what had happened to him overseas intrude on that.

He would fight this. He would.

So he swallowed his hesitation and entered the NICU. It was so hard to hold himself back from wrapping his arms around Ingrid, from pulling her tight against him and kissing her, so instead of doing that he jabbed his hands in the pockets of his jeans.

"Hey," he whispered. "How long have you been waiting?"

Ingrid shrugged and didn't look at him. "I don't know. What time is it?"

"Eight. My shift just ended."

"A few hours, I guess," Ingrid whispered. Her hand was in the incubator, touching their son's arm. "Dr. Steane said that Jase is doing well and they're going to take him off the ventilator tomorrow if his chest films look good."

A lump formed in his throat and he cleared it. "That's good. Does that mean I have to work faster on the room?"

Ingrid sighed. "I wish. They have to slowly wean him off the oxygen and he's been losing weight. He'll have to get up to his birth weight again."

"I'm a trauma surgeon, not a pediatrician or neonatologist."

"I'm aware of that. That was quite a...quite a surgery today."

His blood froze. "Yeah, a police officer shot in the line of duty during a bungled robbery."

"Yeah." Though he knew from the look in her eyes she didn't believe him. She had seen his hesitation and he didn't

know what he was going to say to her. How do you begin
to explain that? He didn't even remember all the horror.

It only came in flashes.

He tried not to think about it, because he didn't want
to dwell on it.

Who would want to dwell on something like that? And
he resented it that he had to.

Life sucked.

"I'm going to pump and then we can go." Ingrid stood
up slowly.

She walked out of the NICU into one of the pump rooms,
leaving Clint alone with Jase. The small room they were
in was quiet except for the sound of the monitors and the
hum of the ventilator breathing for his son.

He turned and looked at the incubator, something he'd
been trying to avoid since he'd entered the NICU, but now
he couldn't help it.

He was drawn to it.

Clint placed his hand on the incubator and stared down
at his son.

Jase.

The name on the tag said Jase Walton. Not Allen.

He leaned in closer to take a look at his son. It was hard
to see anything over the ventilator. There were cords, cath-
eters and a feeding tube. His son was just this tiny little
person wrapped up in a bundle of cords.

He didn't even know the color of his son's eyes because
he'd been sedated since being put on the ventilator.

"You can touch him."

Clint turned and saw Ingrid behind him, smiling.

"Didn't you just leave?"

"I've been gone for thirty minutes."

Thirty minutes?

"Why did you pick the name Jase? Is it a family name?"

"Nope." Ingrid smiled. "It's a derivative of Jason and it

means healer. I thought it was appropriate that the son of two surgeons be named that."

"Good choice."

"Do you want to touch him?"

Clint cleared his throat again. "Uh, I'm not sure."

Ingrid took his hand in her soft, small one. It took his breath away. She pumped some hand sanitizer into his palm and helped him rub his hands together.

His blood heated.

Another emotional response evoked.

Ingrid was breaking through his anesthesia. Soon he would feel pain and he wasn't sure if he was ready for that. He should pull away from her, but he couldn't.

She guided his hand in through the opening, pushing his arm as it extended through, and when his finger touched the warm, soft flesh of his son, he felt pain and joy. All those emotions he'd learned to hide and bury deep within himself as the insurgents had tried to break him.

By all rights, Jase shouldn't be alive, but he'd beaten the odds. Suddenly Clint didn't see a bundle of wires and tubing. There was life in his veins.

Pure. Untainted life.

Jase wasn't broken yet, but his father was.

Ingrid gasped as she shot upright, but that was hard to do when you were only two weeks post-op from a C-section.

The sound that had stirred her from her sleep was gone. The only sound was the howling wind. Maybe it was just something in her dream that had woken her up.

So she relaxed. She needed as much sleep as she could get before Jase was discharged home.

As soon as her head hit the pillow again a scream rent the night, making her heart palpitate and setting off an adrenaline rush.

The scream came again. It was ear-piercing and it echoed

through the house. It sent a chill down her spine. Because it was Clint who was screaming, the noise coming from inside the house.

She got out of bed, bracing her incision site and pulled on her robe.

It was a clear night and the moon filtered through the skylight.

The scream pierced the air again.

And it caused a shudder to move through her. Cold dread.

She moved as fast as she could up the loft stairs, but when she got to the top she couldn't see Clint. The room was cast in shadows.

"Clint?"

She was whacked from behind and fell to her knees.

Clint moved past her, back to the bed. Screaming and thrashing.

Oh, my God.

She was okay. She was fine. The whack had caught her off guard, but she was okay.

"Clint?"

"No!" he screamed. "No."

"Clint!" She moved toward the bed and held him down as he thrashed. "Clint!"

He froze. "Ingrid?"

Thank God.

"Ingrid, what're you doing here?"

"You were screaming." She let go of him.

"I was?"

"Yes."

"Why are you holding me?" he asked.

"You hit me."

His body tensed again under her hands. "Are you okay?"

"I'm fine." She rubbed the back of her head. "I'm okay."

"Good. I'm glad. Now get out."

"Are you sure—?"

"I'm fine. Get out."

Ingrid nodded and left his room. He'd said he was fine. That it was just a nightmare, but she didn't believe him.

She wanted to help him, but it was impossible to help someone who didn't want it, and maybe that was for the best. She had no business helping him.

They shared a child, a roof and that was all.

And that was all it could ever be.

CHAPTER FOURTEEN

"YOU KNOW, WHEN you get eight weeks off on paid medical leave you're not supposed to spend all your time here! You were discharged two months ago." Phil was, of course, teasing as she reached down and stroked Jase's cheek as he rooted toward her. "Now, how am I going to get my cuddle times when my shift is slow? How can you be going home today?"

Ingrid knew that last remark hadn't been directed at her at all. It had been to Jase and she couldn't blame Phil one bit.

The only thing she could argue about was the home comment.

Living at Clint's home wasn't really a home. Just a place to stay.

Ever since that night he'd had the night terror, Clint had been distant and closed off to her.

It was like they were strangers passing in the halls. Clint didn't even sleep at home anymore. He took on more shifts at the hospital, and if she was at the hospital, he'd be back at the ranch and working on the house.

It made for long eight weeks. Two months of awkward and polite silence.

Jase's room was ready for him. It was a beautiful room and it connected to hers. He'd even brought all of the baby stuff she'd bought into the room.

"You're cleared to drive, right? Or is Clint taking you two home?"

"Uh-huh," Ingrid replied.

Though all she knew for certain was the fact she could drive herself. She had no idea if Clint would be here when Jase was finally discharged.

She didn't know what was going on with him.

Though she was positive Clint was suffering from PTSD. She wasn't a psych major, but she recognized the signs. If he had it and was closing people off and having night terrors, why didn't he seek professional help?

Was Clint ashamed?

Though she didn't know why he should be. Something had happened to him over there and she wanted to help him.

"Which is it?" Phil asked, confused.

"Clearance," Ingrid muttered. She cleared her throat. "I have clearance. I don't know if Clint will be coming. He was working and…" She trailed off, trying to think of some excuse because she didn't want to talk about what was going on between them. Not that they had a relationship anyway.

She didn't want to tell Phil about the awkward conversations. How he avoided eye contact with her. Clint was physically there but emotionally he wasn't, and she felt so alone.

Some stupid part of her brain had told her that moving in with Clint was going to be good. That she wouldn't be doing this on her own, like she would've done if she'd stayed with her roommates.

Only that hadn't been the case.

She was just as alone as ever and it terrified her.

How the heck was she going to manage?

What if something happened to Jase, something she couldn't control? It terrified her, it made her anxious. Ingrid didn't like the feeling of losing control.

It was her number-one pet peeve.

"Well, I guess you're not going home alone after all."
Phil grinned and nodded to the door. Ingrid turned to see
Clint standing there. He was dressed casually in a leather
coat, denim trousers and a gray V-neck shirt that brought
out the sparkle in his blue, blue eyes. Those damn eyes,
which had seduced her and sucked her in, held her again.
Enrapturing her.

Dammit.

It had been his eyes that had got her into trouble in the
first place. She had to look away and then her gaze tracked
down and she saw in his hand the car seat she'd bought and
then forgotten at home. He'd remembered.

"Has he been discharged yet?" Clint asked, setting down
the car seat and taking off his jacket.

"N-no, he hasn't." Heat flushed her cheeks and she
turned away like some shy schoolgirl.

"Well, I'll leave you guys." Phil cleared her throat and
moved away. "I'll visit you soon."

"I'll be back to work next week. I'll hopefully find a
sitter for Jase soon."

"I have one lined up," Clint interrupted.

Ingrid spun around, shocked. She could see Phil's brows
arch in surprise.

"You did what?" she asked, her voice raising an octave.

"I think that's my cue to exit stage left." Phil shot her
an encouraging grin and left the NICU.

"Do you think she was running away?" Clint was trying to defuse the tension by making a joke, but after eight
weeks of silence she wasn't in a jovial mood.

Ingrid crossed her arms. "What do you mean, you've
handled it?"

"What?"

"Don't play dumb with me. I mention getting a sitter or a
nanny and you say you've handled it. I want to know how."

Clint ran a hand through his hair, causing it to stick

straight up. "You're going back to work next week and you hadn't even started to look. So I handled it."

Ingrid pinched the bridge of her nose. "Okay, but you still haven't told me much. I mean, I don't know this person. How can I leave my baby with a stranger?"

"Do you think so little of me?"

"I don't know what to think. You haven't spoken two civil words to me in weeks."

Clint sighed. "I'm sorry."

"Apology accepted." Ingrid relaxed. "Thank you for bringing the car seat."

"You're welcome." Clint moved toward the crib and looked down at Jase, who was sleeping peacefully. She watched him for some sign of softness, but there was nothing. The wall, which she had thought was down for just a moment, was back up again. He glanced at his watch. "Hopefully they'll be by soon so we can get you both home to rest."

"So tell me more about this...person you've hired."

"She came highly recommended by Dr. Steane. She's a personal support worker who has dealt with children who have had respiratory issues."

Ingrid was impressed. "When did you talk to Dr. Steane? I've never seen you in here."

"When you were at my house and I was working the night shift. I would check on him and Dr. Steane and I got to talking." She was shocked. He hadn't told her. Of course, he'd barely said anything to her lately.

"I'm impressed. Still, I would've liked to meet..."

"Doris Malone."

"Doris."

Clint nodded. "I know that I overstepped my bounds. I know, but you needed someone and you weren't really looking."

Ingrid nodded again. "I know. I was so overwhelmed by it all."

"This has been a crazy few months." A small smile crept on his lips. "Actually, I think we moved on from the realms of crazy to insanity."

She chuckled. "You can say that again."

"Ah, good, you're both here." Dr. Steane and a couple of his residents entered the room. He nodded and acknowledged them both. "Are you ready to take your son home, Dr. Walton?"

"I am." Though her voice caught in her throat at the thought. No one was ever really ready or prepared, and even though she was a doctor, trained and capable of taking care of a baby who'd had a rough start in life, she was still not ready. But she had to sink all those thoughts of self-doubt; there was no place for them.

Not today.

Dr. Steane began writing in the chart. "I'm very confident after talking to both you and Dr. Allen that your son is able to go home. He's been off the vent for two weeks and the NG tube was removed a week ago and he's had no problem feeding. His weight is back up to his birth weight and other than a small hole in his heart that Cardio isn't concerned about at the moment I'm fairly confident the two of you can take care of him."

"Of course," Clint said, but his brow was furrowed and Ingrid's stomach knotted. She hoped he wasn't having second thoughts, that he wouldn't turn around and boot them out, telling her she was on her own.

He's just hired a nanny. One with peds experience. Would he really do that if he was planning to kick you to the curb?

And then a flashback hit her.

A memory that had been stuck deep in her brain.

She was peering through her father's leaded glass window from his study and on the street was her mother, though she couldn't clearly make out her face because she couldn't remember it.

What she did remember was the rain pattering against the roof, her mother's suitcases scattered on the ground, her mother on her knees and her face buried in her hands.

And that memory, though fleeting, rocked her to her very core.

Ingrid's father had always told her that her mother had left. That her mother hadn't wanted either of them anymore. Had her father lied to her?

She shook the thought away. Even if her father had been lying, why hadn't her mother tried to come back? Why hadn't she fought for her?

"Ingrid?" Clint asked. "Are you okay? You kind of zoned out there for a moment."

Ingrid noticed Dr. Steane and his residents were staring at her as well. "Sorry. What were you saying?"

"I was just explaining that we want Jase to have a follow-up in a week." Dr. Steane held out the discharge papers. "You're free to take him home. Good day, Doctors."

"Okay." Ingrid nodded, taking the papers from Dr. Steane, but she was still shaking. "That sounds good."

Dr. Steane and the other medical personnel left the room.

"Are you okay?" Clint asked again. "You look like you've seen a ghost or something."

Ingrid nodded. "Fine. Let's just get back to...your place and get settled."

She'd almost said home, but it wasn't her permanent home. It would never be.

Right now she didn't have that.

All she had was Jase.

The drive back to the ranch was tense and awkward, as the last few weeks had been. Clint had clammed up again, but it was hard to carry on a conversation when you were in the back, next to a car seat.

When she'd got Jase settled into his crib, Ingrid wanted to have a nap. Clint told her that he was headed back to the hospital and that there was a problem with the pipes, so the only bathroom functioning was in the loft.

Then he was gone and she crashed.

When she woke up, Jase was still sleeping.

Now was the time to sneak a shower.

Ingrid collected what she needed, trying not to blunder about, but her brain was foggy as she careened out of her room and toward the loft.

She wasn't looking as she pushed open the bathroom door and stumbled into a steamy, brightly lit room.

As her eyes adjusted to the light, she saw a very naked and wet Clint standing in front of the mirror. His back was to her and she gasped, seeing him. His back was scarred from the top of his shoulders down to over his backside.

His eyes widened in surprise and their gazes locked in the mirror.

"Leave," he said, his voice strained as he grabbed a towel from the counter and wrapped it around his waist. He turned to face her, his blue eyes dark and unreadable.

Clint took a step toward her and she saw his chest was as scarred as his back. His towel was slung precariously low and she could feel her cheeks heat with the rush of blood and arousal.

Scarred or not, he was still dead sexy.

Before she knew what was happening, his arms were around her. Big, strong arms and she was pressed against his chest. His skin was making her silk camisole damp, his large hand on her throat as he tilted her chin with his thumb and crushed her lips with his in a kiss that made her toes curl.

Her knees went weak and she sank into his kiss. How

she remembered this kiss, had longed for it, but before she could relax and enjoy it he tore his lips away and held her at arm's length.

"Get out," he said. "Before I forget myself and why you're here."

Ingrid turned and left, shutting the door between them before retreating to the safety of her own room.

Though there wasn't much protection when there was only four small walls keeping them apart and she wasn't sure she wanted protection from Clint.

CHAPTER FIFTEEN

HE WAS TRYING to pretend to drink a cup of coffee and read a newspaper, but instead he was watching her as she puttered around the kitchen. Jase was in his swing, staring cross-eyed at a dangling monkey as Ingrid got herself breakfast.

She was nervous. He could sense it.

Though he didn't blame her in the slightest.

It had been a week since their run-in in his bathroom.

Though the way he felt, the way his blood heated every time he saw her, it felt like mere seconds ago he'd had her in his arms again. Lips locked and her curves pressed against his chest. Her nipples pebbling under the silky camisole she'd been wearing.

Her pulse hammering against his thumb as he'd held her slender neck.

He'd had a plumber out the next day to fix the shower in her en suite.

It was safer that way.

Only it wasn't, because he thought about it constantly.

How she had been right next to him. There for the taking if he'd only taken a chance.

And during the week, watching her with Jase had only made the temptation that much greater. Though he'd heard her complaining once, over the phone, that she wasn't happy with her body and how clothes didn't fit, Clint saw nothing wrong with her newfound voluptuousness.

Her body hadn't altered that much and as he took in her shape, tilting his head, he could see she only benefited by the slight widening of her hips and the larger swell to her breasts. The birth of the baby had given her one of those classic hourglass shapes. The kind Jean Harlow or Marilyn Monroe would have been envious of.

He liked curves on a woman.

"What time did Doris say she was coming?"

Clint shook his head and ripped his gaze from her figure before she turned around and caught him staring at her behind, which was wrapped up in a tight pencil skirt. He cleared his throat and straightened his paper, flipping the page, not even sure what he was reading because the words looked like jumbled nonsense to him.

"She should be here soon."

Ingrid cocked an eyebrow. "'Soon' is not a definitive time."

Clint shrugged. "She'll be here on time. Don't stress."

"Yeah, right." Ingrid sighed and continued packing her attaché case.

He snuck a glance at her over the top of his paper. She was dressed professionally, but he knew today was consult day for her. She wouldn't be on call. Today would be the day she'd be visiting patients who would be booking surgery with her.

Her golden hair was done up in a French twist, which was a shame. He preferred it loose and hanging down over her shoulders or even gently twisted around his fist while he took her from behind.

Clint cleared his throat and rustled his paper. He shouldn't be thinking like this, but he couldn't help it.

It had been on his mind since that night she'd stumbled into his bathroom.

He'd thought she'd used it while he'd been back at the hospital. He hadn't expected a midnight visitor.

Clint set down the paper and stood. "Ingrid, do you want to have dinner with me tonight?"

She spun around and her mouth dropped open. Even he was shocked as the words spilled from his mouth.

This was not keeping her at emotional arm's length.

This was the exact opposite of what he was trying to achieve, but he couldn't help himself. He was weak when it came to her.

"Pardon?" she said, blinking a few times.

"Dinner. With me."

"What about Jase?"

"We can pay Doris a little bit of overtime. You're off at four and so am I. We can have an early dinner. Go straight from the hospital."

Ingrid's eyes were still wide as she took a sip of her coffee. "You have it all figured out, then. How long have you been thinking about this?"

"Does it matter?" Clint asked.

A sly smile spread across her lips. "If you want an answer from me."

He got up and moved toward her. "That's blackmail."

Ingrid was going to open her mouth and say more, but the doorbell rang. "That must be Doris. I'll let her in."

She tried to walk away, but he grabbed her wrist. "You didn't give me an answer."

The doorbell rang again. It was cold outside, but he didn't care. He wasn't going to let her go without an answer. Yes or no. Part of him wanted her to say no, it would be easier, but the other part of him wanted a yes. Needed a yes.

"Fine. I'll go out with you."

Clint let go of her hand so she could answer the door.

What have I got myself into?

She could see Clint across the E.R. and he was working on a patient, but it didn't seem to be such an emergency.

Which was good. It would mean that he would be on time for dinner.

Then she looked down and saw that she wasn't exactly dressed for a date.

Was it a date?

No, it wasn't a date. It was just dinner. A thank-you for having his baby.

Yes. It was an appreciation dinner.

And that's what she had to keep reminding herself. There was nothing between them. There couldn't be.

Ingrid went through the rest of her consults and tried not to think about it, but it was hard. She hadn't been on a date in a long, long time.

What if she'd forgotten how to date?

Any time she'd had a previous date, well, they hadn't gone well.

The one and only time a date had gone well had been the night she'd conceived Jase.

Lord. Sometimes her life was a bit of a joke.

She finished her last chart and set it back at the nurses' station. In her very near future, she would have surgeries to perform.

Surgery was what she loved to do and she couldn't wait to get her hands back in the O.R. To feel bone. To have a drill in her hand and replace a knee.

Consults were all well and good, but there was nothing like getting your hands dirty. Bloody. That's what she wanted.

Instead, she was standing at the charge station, wondering if she looked okay when she should've been worried about O.R. schedules and whether Jase was okay.

Which he was. She'd called Doris.

There was no way she could go out to dinner. Just no way.

She had to find some excuse, because going out alone

with him was dangerous. It was putting her heart at risk and she'd sworn she'd never put her heart on the line like that for anyone.

As she turned around Clint came toward her. He wasn't in his scrubs. He was in jeans, a sports blazer and a white shirt, which wasn't buttoned all the way.

His black hair was neatly combed, but he had five o'clock shadow and he looked tired. Like any new parent.

She was positive she had bags under her eyes. She could feel them. Like giant sandbags, and she was sure she smelled like sour milk.

Stop thinking about it.

Clint stopped in front of her. "You ready to go?"

No. Think of something. Only she couldn't.

"Sure. I just finished up the last of my charts." Ingrid grabbed her purse and her jacket from where she'd left them. "Where are we going?"

Clint nodded. "Somewhere."

She followed him as they walked down the hall and tried not to roll her eyes at his evasive behavior.

She followed him in silence out to the car and remained silent as they drove across the city to a small Italian restaurant, all tucked away behind some old buildings in the downtown core. He got out of the car and opened her door for her.

"I don't think I've been here before," Ingrid remarked as they walked toward the restaurant door.

Clint cocked an eyebrow. "Really?" He held open the door.

Ingrid sighed as she stepped inside. "I'm getting tired of these one-word answers."

He grinned. "Are you going to blackmail me to get longer answers?"

"It wasn't blackmail."

"Sounded like blackmail to me." He turned to the seating hostess. "Reservation for Allen."

The seating hostess grinned and grabbed two menus. "Follow me."

They followed her to the back, where she led them to a booth tucked in the corner.

Once they were seated Ingrid pled her case. "I wasn't blackmailing you. I'm trying to get to know you. I'm so tired of the silence. We may be roommates, but we share a child together. I'd like us to be friends."

"Just friends?" he asked, and she wondered if there was a hint of disappointment in his voice.

Did he want more?

Well, it didn't matter because she couldn't give him more.

"Yes, friends working together to raise our son in an open and caring environment."

"I can live with that." He took a sip of water. "But I'm not the only one being silent."

"I'm an open book."

Clint snorted and tented his fingers. "Are you? Then why don't you tell me about your parents? Why is your father such a jerk?"

Ingrid laughed. "You're not exactly forthcoming about your parents. Why haven't you told your parents about Jase?"

"You go first."

Ingrid grinned. "Fine, but you'd better order a big bottle of wine."

"You're breastfeeding."

"I pumped earlier. I get wine."

Clint motioned to the waitress and ordered a bottle of red. Once the bottle was uncorked the waitress poured only one glass.

"You're not drinking?"

"No, I don't drink." Clint leaned back. "Only water for me. And I was only teasing before. You can have wine. As long as you don't feed Jase for four hours and I suggest only one glass."

"Deal. Now spill."

"Nice try, Dr. Walton. I believe I asked you first. What is up with your father?"

Ingrid chuckled and pinched the stem of her wineglass. "I've been wondering about that myself for almost thirty years."

"He told me he brought you up to be independent. Well, those weren't exactly his words, but that's the gist I got."

"That's about right. I had to take responsibility for all my actions. I guess in a way it helped me grow up to be a critical thinker. I never took risks, and thought before I made any decision in my life."

Clint cocked his brows. "What did you think about the night we met, then? I'm curious about your thought process."

She blushed. "That was one of the two only decisions in my life where I didn't think things through and just went for it."

And look where it got me. Only she kept that thought to herself.

"One of the two. What was the other one?"

"Keeping Jase."

He dropped his gaze and smiled. "That was a good decision."

Ingrid watched him. "You think so?"

Clint met her gaze. Those dark rims around the blue were darker and making her heart beat just a bit faster. "I know so."

She blushed and looked away. "I'm glad you're happy and I'm glad you're involved."

Clint nodded. "I'm trying to be. I really am. There is…
I know I build up walls."

"No kidding." The she sighed. "Sorry, I didn't mean to
be so sarcastic."

"No, it's okay. I deserved that."

"Well, I have my own walls too, but you have to build
them sometimes. It's just easier to keep people out than
let them in."

Which was true. Something her father had taught her.
Then again, she wasn't sure what to believe anymore.

"You never talk about your mother. Tell me about her."

Ingrid took a sip of wine and shrugged. "There's nothing to tell. She left and didn't want me."

"What makes you think that?"

Ingrid rolled her eyes. "Because she's never tried to
make contact. Even when I became an adult."

"Perhaps she was scared."

Ingrid pursed her lips as the thought processed through
her mind and she put herself in her mother's shoes. What
if it was Jase and her? What if she'd been forced to leave
Jase behind? What if she was too scared to contact Jase
when he became a legal adult?

She shook her head at the ridiculousness of it all because
she would never, ever do that.

She'd never let cowardice get in her way.

Only you do.

Ingrid cleared her throat. "What about your family? Why
haven't you told them about your return?"

"Way to change the subject."

"It's tit for tat, dude."

"I'll gladly show you my tat," he drawled, his voice deep
and brushing over her skin like smooth velvet.

Focus.

"Don't change the subject."

Clint groaned and leaned back. "I'm not ready to tell them about what happened to me."

"What did happen to you?"

Clint's brow furrowed. "That wasn't the question I agreed on."

"Do they think you're injured or something, because if they do it's pretty awful of you to leave them hanging on."

Clint scrubbed a hand over his face. "No, they know I got out okay. They just think I'm over in Germany…rehabilitating."

"From what?" Ingrid's stomach knotted and she recalled the way his body was scarred. When they had been together before he'd gone overseas there hadn't been a mark on him and when she'd seen him the bathroom…well, it was too horrible for her to contemplate.

"I was captured," he said, his voice tense. "Captured and tortured."

Ingrid's hand rose to her neck. "Oh, my God, but you were a medic."

"I was an American. It didn't matter to them, but I think being a doctor helped me out."

"How's that?"

"They kept me alive to treat their wounded. The others…" Clint shook his head. "In those few months I was there, let's just say I've seen enough blood shed to last a lifetime."

Ingrid reached out and touched his hand. "I'm sorry."

The waitress came back and they ordered from her. Once the waitress left a tense silence descended between them and Ingrid could feel the wine going to straight to her head. She'd been a lightweight drinker anyway and not having any kind of alcohol for over a year just made it work faster.

She set down her wineglass.

"Are you okay?" Clint asked. "Your face is flushed."

"The wine is going to my head. I'm not used to it."

He poured a glass of ice water from the carafe into her glass. "Drink that. It'll help."

"Thanks." She drank the water quickly and set the glass down. "So how did you escape your imprisonment?"

Clint kissed his teeth. "We're back to that again, eh?"

"I'm curious."

Clint licked his lips and she could tell by the expression on his face he was thinking and that made her nervous. How bad had his capture been? She'd seen the physical scars on his body. Those had healed, but it was the ones down deep he was struggling with. She knew it.

"I escaped through some old sewer pipes. They hunted me through the sewers, but I got out. Eventually." Clint rolled his neck. The word "eventually" had stuck, like he'd had to think hard about it, and then she understood why he'd turned an old ranch house into an open-concept home. Why he lived in such a spacious loft with high ceilings and skylights.

"How long were you trapped in the sewers?"

"I don't want to talk about that."

Ingrid shook her head. "I'm sorry. I know you've been dealing with post-traumatic stress disorder and—"

"What?" Clint asked, his eyes dark. "Who said I was dealing with PTSD?"

"Well, it's obvious."

Clint cocked his head to one side. "How is it obvious?"

"The nightmares, the emotional walls and that time in surgery when you froze."

His gaze was intense. "You saw that."

"Yes."

Clint cursed under his breath. "I don't like surgery anymore. I just want to own a ranch. I can't be a surgeon any longer than I have to."

"I don't understand."

"They made me operate on people who were not sedated.

There's only so many times you can listen to the screams before you realize you're just a butcher and no longer the healer you wanted to be."

Ingrid could see him visibly shaking. A wall was crumbling and she wasn't sure if she had what it took to keep him from toppling down with it.

"Clint, you are a healer. You are not a butcher."

He snorted. "I froze in surgery. I loved being a surgeon, but now...no, I do more harm than good."

She reached across the table and took his hand, which was shaking. "I don't know how you can say that. You save lives. The people you help now need it. You're a trauma surgeon. They'd die without you."

Clint was going to say something further, but the waitress brought them their food. All he did was push her hand away and that was the end of the discussion.

The rest of the dinner was tense and Ingrid regretted prying, but she wanted to know.

She needed to know and she wanted to help him.

Badly.

You're going to get hurt.

She told that part of her to shut up. At this precise moment she simply didn't care.

CHAPTER SIXTEEN

THE CRYING INFILTRATED his dreams and Clint woke with a start. His heart was racing and it took him a few moments to orientate himself. To realize that he was in his room.

He was in his big, open bedroom. High ceilings where he could see the sky through the skylight and as he looked up he could see stars twinkling in the inky blackness. So brilliant and enhanced by the cold.

Heat reminded him of overseas.

The bitter cold of a South Dakota winter reminded him that he was no longer someone's prisoner. That he was home.

He was safe.

Only the winter would end soon. It was almost April and spring would come. Then summer, which would bring the dry, arid heat of the badlands.

He planned to spend his summer in a lot of air-conditioning, which wouldn't be good for him. Which could cause colds, but he was willing to be dealt that. If he was hot during the night, it would trigger the flashbacks and he had to keep those under control.

As his pulse rate returned to normal, he lay back down in his bed, but the moment his head hit the pillow the small cry filtered up the stairs from down below.

The only downside to having one's bedroom in a loft— there was no door, no walls to drown out the sounds of the rest of the house, but he just couldn't sleep in a confined room.

It was why he also had a king-size mattress.

He needed space. In his sleep he needed to be able to reach out and not touch anything. He needed to feel like he wasn't trapped in a coffin or a pipe.

A shudder ran down his spine.

Don't think about that.

When he'd built Jase's room he hadn't even been able to finish the walls or the ceiling. Jase's room was basically four walls. Like a really fancy cubicle with a door. The only room that was closed off was Ingrid's, but that was because it had been there when he'd bought the house. Renovating it and her bathroom had been a challenge. Of course, his hatred for confined spaces and his need/love for open spaces was why Ingrid had walked in on him when he had just gotten out of the shower.

He could still see the pink rise to the surface of her skin as she'd looked away, before she'd bolted. Of course, he had told her to leave, even though he had wanted her to come in and join him.

He'd been thinking about her when she'd walked in on him.

It was hard not to think about her. She was constantly on his mind. Ever since that night he'd accidentally hit her, he'd been terrified.

Terrified of all the feelings she brought out in him and terrified of hurting her more badly. Ingrid was not his.

But she could be.

Clint shook his head and covered his eyes with the back of his arm. He couldn't think that way.

He'd let down his guard once and he'd hit her because she'd been concerned about him screaming in the night.

She'd just had surgery too. He could've done real damage to her and then how would he be able to live with himself?

Only you didn't do any damage.

He groaned and rolled over on his stomach. The baby began to cry again, louder, and Clint knew he wouldn't be getting any sleep.

He climbed out of bed and pulled on his jeans, before heading down the loft stairs to Jase's room.

When he opened the door, he stopped dead in his tracks at the sight he saw. Something he wasn't prepared for emotionally.

Ingrid was in the rocking chair, her golden hair down, and in her arms was her son. His son.

Their son.

And she was rocking him while he fed.

The moonlight filtering through the skylight made her pale skin glow. It was like he had suddenly stepped into some kind of fairy ring and she was Titania. Her skin was radiant, her hair sparkled like gold had been woven into each strand and he couldn't help but stare at them.

Mother and son.

It wasn't long before Jase went back to sleep and, instead of just the creamy white tops of her breast, Clint could see it all.

Her breasts were fuller since the last time he'd seen them, but they were still beautiful and just the thought of touching her made his blood heat.

He wanted her.

More than anything.

You can't have her.

Only he could. She was right here and he knew somewhere, deep down that if he only reached out to her, she'd be his. Even if he didn't deserve it.

She covered her breast and laid Jase back in his crib. When she turned around to leave she gasped when she saw him.

"Clint?" she whispered. "You scared me half to death. What're you doing here?"

He could have said "I heard a cry" or said "I was just watching you" but instead his brain let his other head do the talking and he said, "God help me, but at this moment I want you again."

Clint braced himself for the backlash. The rejection. The outrage.

Instead, she raised her hand and placed it on her chest, her long slender fingers just brushing the hollow of her neck.

"What?" It was barely more than a whisper. "I—I thought you were mad at me."

Clint closed the gap between them. "No, I wasn't mad at you. Okay, I was a little, but… I don't want to talk about that. I just want you, Ingrid."

He tipped her chin and ran his knuckles down over her cheek, feeling gooseflesh break out across her skin. He was having an effect on her, just like she was affecting him.

Her long lashes brushed the tops of her cheeks.

She was so beautiful.

"I want you, too," she said, in barely a whisper. "Though I shouldn't, though I've tried to deny it."

It was all the answer Clint needed. He didn't want to discuss things further. He just wanted to be with her. Touch her. Kiss her. Taste her.

He wanted her to chase the ghosts away. He wanted to feel alive again, even if for just a short time.

Clint scooped her up in his arms. Her arms came around his neck, her slender fingers tangling in the hair at the nape of his neck. He carried her to his room, to his bed, because he didn't want to have a claustrophobic moment.

Not with her. Not right now.

No words were needed as he moved up the steps, moonlight the only thing lighting his way to his bedroom. He set her down on her feet in front of him.

"You're so beautiful," he murmured, as he cupped her face with his hands and pressed his lips against her and she melted into him.

The last time they'd been together it had been fast, hot and heavy. This time he wanted to take things slowly with her. He didn't want to hurt her and he wanted to savor this moment, because all the time he'd been captured and even when he'd been in Germany, convincing the whole world that he was okay, it was the memories of her that had pulled him through.

Now that he had her again, it scared him that he was going to lose himself in her, that he would hurt her. If he did that it would kill him.

If he was whole he'd drop down on his knees and give all of himself to her, but he was broken and he doubted that he would ever be whole again.

So for this moment he would savor it while he could.

Clint let his hands drift from her cheeks down to her shoulders and where her simple white cotton nightgown was held up by two ties. He pushed her satin housecoat off and then pulled on the ties of her nightgown.

She let out a moan and bit her lip.

"What's wrong?" He asked.

"I don't want you to see me naked." There was a warm flush to her cheeks. She was embarrassed and was looking away from him.

He tipped her chin so she was looking at him. "You're beautiful. We've both changed physically, but you're sexy and I want to see you."

Ingrid's eyes sparkled in the darkness and she kissed him again, pressing her soft body against his, trying to meld the two of them together.

Clint undid her nightgown and it fell to the floor. He

broke the connection and trailed his mouth down her neck, the flutter of her pulse heating his blood further, and when his kiss traveled down over her breasts she gasped.

"Did I hurt you?" he murmured against her ear, drinking in the scent of her.

"No." Ingrid moved and sat down on his bed, taking his hand and pulling him closer. "Make love to me, Clint. Please."

She didn't need to ask him, but it made his body thrum with excitement that she did. Ingrid reached out and undid his jeans, tugging them down so he was naked. He kicked them off and then reached into a drawer for protection and hoped that what had happened to them the last time didn't happen again, because it was way too soon for Ingrid to even contemplate getting pregnant again.

And that thought terrified him.

Why was he even contemplating having another child with her?

"Clint?"

He turned to her and she took the condom packet from his hand.

"What're you doing?" he asked.

Only she didn't answer him, she kept her gaze locked on his, her eyes like diamonds in the darkness as she opened the package and rolled it over his erection. The moment her fingers touched his shaft he almost lost it.

It had been so long. She had been the last woman he had been with and he thought that she would be the last forever, because he was damaged inside. His body trembled as her hands stroked his abdomen.

He let her pull him down on the bed beside her. They lay down together and he ran his hands over her body slowly, not wanting to hurt her.

And when he slid her underwear off she bit her lip. She'd healed from her surgery, but it was a reminder of what their last time together had brought about and she tried to cover the small scar that ran horizontally just below her hips.

"Don't hide yourself from me. You're beautiful."

And he kissed her again, her legs opening up to welcome his weight. He kept the connection as he entered her. She cried out as he stretched her, filled her completely.

He braced his weight on one arm as he began to move, her body stretched out beneath him, and he stroked her long, slender neck.

Ingrid was so vulnerable to him.

Sex was about trust and this ultimate act between them made him want to protect her forever. He wanted her to tear down all the walls he'd built to protect himself, but he'd built them too high and he was scared to allow them to come down.

Her nails raked across his back as he increased his speed.

The only sound was their breathing as they moved together, joined and fused.

Ingrid bit her lip as she tightened around his erection, her body releasing as her orgasm moved through her. It didn't take him long before he followed her. Allowing pent-up emotion to surge through him, he threw back his head, his hands on her hips, holding her tight against his body as he came.

It took her a moment for her breathing to return to normal.

Clint moved off her and moved to the side, his head propped up on one elbow. She could feel him watching her. Then with his free hand he brushed his knuckles over her breasts.

"I should get back to bed." Ingrid tried to get up, but he gently held her down.

"No, stay the night."

"What if Jase cries?"

"Stay here." Clint got out of bed and she watched him

as he walked naked across the loft and disappeared down the stairs.

He was only gone for a couple of minutes before he returned with the baby monitor. He set it down on the nightstand by the bed and climbed back, leaning back against his pillows.

"I thought this might convince you to stay the night with me, not that we really need it. I can hear him quite easily through the house."

Ingrid smiled and climbed in under the covers beside him. "Yes, well, I understand your love of open spaces now."

When she lay back against the pillows she could see the large skylight over his bed. She hadn't noticed it before because she'd been too preoccupied.

"You should've just built a glass roof with all the skylights you have in here."

Clint chuckled. "I wanted to, but it wasn't feasible in South Dakota. The skylights in the kitchen are standard, but I had this custom-made. I wouldn't be able to sleep any other way."

"How long were you trapped in the sewers?"

"An eternity." He raked his hands through his hair. "A couple of days, and then they finally stopped looking for me. They figured I was dead and I crawled out, disappearing into the crowd. My hair had grown out, I had a beard and I blended in. Finally I was able to find a patrolling unit and they flew me out of there and into Germany."

"I'm sorry." She reached out and touched one of the puckered scars on his chest. "So sorry."

She was expecting him to move her hand away, but he didn't. Instead, he closed his hand over the top of hers.

"I don't want to talk about it. I just want to lie here with you. I just want to sleep with you."

Ingrid nodded. "Okay."

She gazed back up at the ceiling. The inky black sky

was mesmerizing and though she couldn't see the moon, she knew it was there, but soon the clear starry sky disappeared as fat, white flakes began to fall.

And that was all she saw as she slipped into a comfortable sleep beside Clint.

Clint couldn't sleep with her curled up beside him. He was afraid to go to sleep. He was afraid the dream was going to come again and that he would hurt her. It terrified him. He didn't want to hurt Ingrid.

So instead he disentangled himself from where she'd curled around him and pulled on some clothes. Just as he was about to head downstairs, he heard Jase.

He glanced back at Ingrid, sleeping soundly, and he didn't want to disturb her. Jase had fed not that long ago, so he wasn't hungry.

You can deal with him. But just the thought of handling his son on his own sent his panic into overdrive. He wasn't good with kids or babies or anything that expelled so many bodily secretions in a day.

He looked back at Ingrid again, sleeping so peacefully.

He could do this. She got up to be with Jase every night, several times a night. He could do this at least once.

Clint turned off the monitor so it wouldn't disturb Ingrid and headed down the stairs into Jase's room.

Jase was still crying, the pitch beginning to rise.

"Hey, I'm here," Clint called out in the darkness. Though the room was lit by a night-light plugged in the wall. "You're not alone."

Jase continued to cry, but it wasn't so urgent now. Clint leaned over the crib and touched Jase's belly, which was quite bloated.

The baby scrunched up his fat little face and cried again, stiffening his legs and arms as he wailed. It was obvious the infant was uncomfortable, but Jase didn't know why.

Well, he should probably start with the bottom.

Gingerly he picked up Jase and carried him over to the change table. He began to unbutton the sleeper, but there were so many buttons it was overwhelming as they snapped apart.

Then Clint caught a whiff and winced.

"Dude, that's terrible."

He grabbed a diaper out of a basket and pulled off the dirty one, breathing through his mouth the entire time. He then pulled out ten wipes and cleaned Jase's bottom. He probably didn't need ten wipes for each time he wiped, but he wanted a big barrier between his son's mess and him.

When his son was sufficiently clean he wrapped up the entire packet of wipes he'd used inside the dirty diaper and dropped it into the trash can, which was next to the change table. Then he slathered some antibacterial gel into his hand, thanking God that it was scented.

After that he attempted to diaper Jase, but that proved to be tricky in itself because his son would not stop kicking and moving.

Finally, he got the diaper on and did it up, but when it came to cramming his son back into the sleeper with a million snaps, Clint gave up.

It was late at night—no, scratch that, it was early in the morning—and there was no way he was going to wrestle with that.

He got it partially done up, even though rolls of fat were still sticking out of the sleeper. He carried Jase back to the crib and laid him down, but Jase started to cry again.

"Okay, I'll pick you up again." Clint held him close and then wandered over to the rocking chair. "How about we rock?"

Jase obviously couldn't answer, but Clint started to rock him and the baby settled, but before he settled he let out a large belch and spit up on Clint's bare shoulder.

Oh, my God. Did that just happen?

Clint grabbed a receiving blanket, wiped up the mess and tossed it into the open hamper. He grabbed a new clean receiving blanket and then settled back down into the rocking chair, putting Jase over his shoulder and rubbing his back.

"Gas pain does suck, but you really didn't need to barf on me."

Though he'd had worse things expelled on him.

Still, even with all the gross things he'd seen in his career as a surgeon, the sour milk barf his son had just yakked on his bare shoulder had to be the worst.

No, the worst had been what had been in his diaper.

"Seriously, how does something so small make so many nasty messes?"

Jase didn't answer, he just sucked on his little curled fist, which was in his mouth. Even though Clint had the receiving blanket as a barrier, he could feel it getting damp.

"Just no more barfing, okay?"

And for good measure Jase burped in response as Clint patted his back, but there was no throw-up. Thankfully.

Clint wasn't sure how long he rocked. Finally, Jase's body relaxed and his head rested on his shoulder, but by then Clint's eyes were closing. He got up and put Jase back into his crib and returned to the rocking chair.

He'd stay here for a few moments. He couldn't go back to bed yet and the chair was comfortable. So he lay his head back and closed his eyes.

He only intended for it to happen for a moment, but as soon as his head hit the plush head cushion he fell into a dreamless sleep.

CHAPTER SEVENTEEN

"OH, MY GOD! You had sex last night, didn't you?" Phil shook her head. "Don't try and deny it, I can see the grin from down the hall. I'm so jealous."

Ingrid chuckled and pulled on her scrub top. "Don't announce it to the whole world."

Even though she really wanted to.

The night with Clint had been wonderful. Of course, when she'd woken up Clint had been missing, which had made her panic and her stupid first thought had been that he'd left.

Of course it was ridiculous. When she'd gone downstairs to Jase's room she'd found Clint asleep in the chair with a soggy receiving blanket plastered to his shoulder. She chuckled to remember that. It had been so cute. When she'd peered in on Jase, she'd had to try and stifle her laughter because her son had been partially dressed and the snaps that had been done up hadn't matched. One leg and one arm on opposite sides of his body had been hanging out and his diaper had been on backwards.

Clint had obviously tried to change him and she loved him for it.

It had been a good attempt and she didn't blame him. Those snaps had been tough for her to figure out in the beginning as well.

She could reconstruct a knee, replace a hip, but baby clothes and diapers had eluded her for a while.

She'd woken Clint and ushered him upstairs to clean him up, but he'd collapsed back into bed and then Jase had woken up. After she'd fed Jase, she'd finally got Clint into the shower where everything had started again.

Something had changed between them, but there were aspects that stayed the same.

Clint had lowered his guard slightly, but there were still many walls between them.

There was still a long way to go, but at least it was progress and Ingrid didn't want to mess it up.

"So tell me, what happened?"

Ingrid shrugged and then pulled on her white lab coat. "We had a nice dinner and things just progressed."

"How was it? Was it good?" Phil snorted and crossed her arms. "Of course it was good from the way you're smiling."

"You're pathetic." Ingrid walked out of the locker room and headed toward the E.R. as she was the orthopedic surgeon on call today.

"Well, I've been so busy that now I have to live vicariously through you."

Ingrid rolled her eyes. "That's what you told me almost a year ago before he knocked me up."

"So sue me." Phil winked. "Well, for what it's worth I'm glad things are going better. There were a few times there I thought you were going to tear his throat out or he was going to bolt."

A shiver of dread traveled down Ingrid's spine when Phil said "bolt," but she shook it off.

"I know, he has a lot going on."

Phil cocked an eyebrow. "And you don't?"

They stopped at the E.R. "Are you on call today?" Ingrid asked.

"No. Actually, I'm off duty. I'm going home to sleep. In

three days, I'm back on day rotation and we'll have to plan a night out together. You can bring Jase."

"Now, what fun would that be?" Ingrid winked at her. "Give me a call."

"Will do." Phil waved as she walked down the hall.

Ingrid took a deep breath and headed into the E.R. It had been some time since she'd been the ortho attending on call and she had to admit it was great being back. Clint was behind the desk, going over some charts, and the E.R. was eerily quiet.

She wandered over to him. "Anything I can help with?"

Clint barely spared her a glance. "No, Dr. Walton. I'll let you know."

It was like a slap to the face. This morning it had been whispered words of affection and her name on his lips.

You're at work.

And as if he was reading her mind, he shut the chart and looked up. "Sorry, I just thought it would be more..."

"I get it, more professional. I understand. Sorry, it's the hormones in me. I can't quite control them yet."

He smiled. "Well, you're going to have to control them in about ten minutes."

"Why?"

Only before he could tell her she heard the distant wail of an ambulance headed their way.

"Got a call about twenty minutes ago that a woman slipped and fell outside her apartment complex and broke her hip. Paramedics say there could be more damage to her. I'm expecting lots of trauma—the temp is hovering around zero and it's snowing. Lots of black ice."

Oh, joy.

The wail of the ambulance became louder and Clint handed her a trauma gown. "We'd better go."

"I'm right behind you, Dr. Allen."

She pulled on her trauma gown and followed him out to meet the ambulance, which had just pulled up.

The door burst open and the two paramedics lifted the gurney down.

"Female age sixty-four slipped on black ice outside her apartment complex. Suspected hip fracture and possible blunt trauma to the head. Patient is complaining of chest pains and her GCS in the field was four."

Clint grabbed the information notes from the paramedic and moved to one side of the gurney, while Ingrid moved to the other side.

The woman's eyes were closed as she breathed in the oxygen from the mask on her face.

"Page Neuro," Clint shouted over the din.

"I need a portable X-ray as well!" Ingrid called out, as she helped push the gurney into a trauma pod.

With the help of the paramedics they lifted her onto a hospital bed and the paramedics took back their gurney.

Clint flipped open the chart the paramedics had provided and gave Ingrid a strange look before turning to the patient. "Mrs. …Walton, you're going to be okay."

Ingrid froze as she stared at the woman. No. It couldn't be. It was just a weird fluke.

The woman groaned. "Just. Heidi."

Ingrid's blood drained from her face and she felt like her stomach was about to leap out of her mouth inside out. Her mother's name was Heidi. Oh, God.

Focus. Maybe she won't recognize you.

"Heidi?" Clint asked.

The woman barely nodded.

"Well, we'll get you some pain meds, Heidi. Hold on. Ingrid, are you okay?" Clint asked.

She rolled her neck. "Perfectly. Would someone get that portable X-ray in here, stat!"

The portable X-ray was wheeled into the room and

Ingrid bent over the woman. "Now, Heidi, I have to move the oxygen mask while we get a good look at what's going on."

The woman's eyes opened and they were blue. So very blue, and Ingrid had a flashback.

Of being rocked in a chair. Her mother's arms around her and bright sunlight filtering behind her mother and clear, blue eyes. Kind eyes that were filled with love and pride.

"Everything will be okay." Ingrid could barely get the words out.

The woman just stared at her like she was looking at a ghost and Ingrid couldn't blame her as she stared at the very fragile injured woman in front of her.

"Who—who are you?" Heidi asked, her voice shaking.

"That's Dr. Walton. Ingrid Walton," Clint said. "Now, if you could remain still, we'll get a picture of your hips and see how bad the damage is."

Focus.

"Right," Ingrid said quickly. She moved away from the woman and pulled the X-ray over to get it ready. "Lie still for me, Heidi." It was hard to get the words out.

As Ingrid prepped the machine, the patient on the table wouldn't tear her gaze from Ingrid and it made her feel a bit uncomfortable.

Ingrid's resident covered Heidi Walton with a protective iron apron, and when it was ready they all stepped out of the room while the machine did its work.

When the pictures had been taken, the same resident wheeled the machine away.

Heidi was still staring at Ingrid and it was unnerving the way the woman was watching her.

Don't look at me. Don't.

Clint was bent over their patient, checking on the rest

of her vitals, while Ingrid felt like a useless lump. She had to get out of there.

"Do—do you need me any further, Dr. Allen?"

Clint glanced up. "No, I think I can stabilize the hip until you get your films back."

Ingrid nodded. "Call if you need me."

She turned on her heel and ran as fast as she could, putting as much distance between herself and that trauma room.

She started to pray that by the time they got all Heidi Walton's other problems sorted out, her shift would be over and she wouldn't have to deal with the woman any longer. Or have another trauma come in. One that was more serious than doing a hip replacement.

What she wouldn't give for a nice, clean amputation right about now.

That's horrible, Ingrid.

She berated herself for thinking that way, but she just couldn't deal with Heidi Walton at the moment. She couldn't deal with her mother. Not now. Not after all this time.

She must've been standing at the charge desk for longer than it felt like because the X-rays were delivered to her.

Ingrid took them into an examination room and threw them on the light box.

Crap.

The woman needed a hip replacement.

There was some bone loss as well.

This was just her lucky day.

"Hey, are those Mrs. Walton's scans?" Clint asked as he came into the room.

"Yep." Ingrid sighed. "She's going to need a hip replacement."

Clint cocked his head to one side. "You don't seem very keen on doing a hip replacement. I thought that you were looking forward to getting your hands dirty?"

Ingrid rubbed the back of her neck. "I am, but you know a hip replacement is so mundane."

"What's going on?" Clint asked suspiciously. "What are you not telling me?"

"Nothing!" She pulled the scans down from the light box and handed them to Clint. "You're the doctor on her file. You need to tell her the news. Once she's stable I'll book an O.R. and get her hip replaced as soon as possible."

"Okay, but you're the ortho attending. I'm sure she'll want to hear it from you."

Ingrid shook her head. "No, it's better you tell her. I have to go."

It was a lie. She had nowhere to go, but she had to stall things.

She had to get out of there as fast as she could, because she wasn't really keen on ghosts. Real or imaginary.

Clint watched her walk away in disbelief.

What had just happened?

He looked down at the X-rays in his hand and then he processed it. Though it wasn't positive and if it was true, something would've been said by now.

There had to be some other reason why Ingrid had bolted. Why she didn't want to do surgery, even if it was just a boring old hip replacement like she had said.

He headed back to the exam room.

Heidi Walton was off the oxygen and the cardio physician on call was just finishing their exam.

"Nothing is wrong with her heart or lungs," Dr. Toneish said. "I think it was the stress of the incident, though her blood pressure is a bit elevated so we'll have to watch for that. Neuro cleared her as well."

"Thank you, Dr. Toneish."

Dr. Toneish nodded and left the trauma pod.

Heidi's gaze landed on him and a shiver crawled down

his spine. He'd seen those eyes, even though they were a slightly different shade, before. He knew that look.

"Where's Dr. Walton?" she asked, her voice hitching slightly.

"She had another patient to attend to." Clint moved to the light box and put the X-rays up. "You have a broken hip, Mrs. Walton—"

"Please, just call me Heidi."

Clint nodded. "Okay, Heidi. You're going to have a hip replacement."

Heidi cursed. "I'm a schoolteacher. I can't afford to miss a day. I just returned to the area so I don't have the best in with the school board."

"Well, I think if I call the board and tell them what happened to you, they'll understand."

Heidi nodded. "I appreciate that, Dr. Allen." She bit her lip, like she wanted to talk further, only nothing came out of her mouth.

"Do you have any further questions, Heidi?"

"Will Dr. Walton be performing my surgery?"

"Most likely. Do you not want her to?" Clint asked.

"Well, no. I mean, she looks like a fairly capable physician."

"She's one of the best. She took on her role as attending orthopedic surgeon quite young and it's very rare for a surgeon of that age to move up so quickly. You'll be in good hands."

Heidi worried her bottom lip. "Is there anyone else who could perform the surgery?"

Clint pulled up a rolling stool so he could look Heidi Walton right in the eye. "Now, why would you ask me something like that?"

Heidi closed her eyes. It was obvious the morphine she'd been given by Ingrid was beginning to kick in as she muttered some nonsensical stuff.

"Heidi," Clint said, leaning over. "Is there a reason why Dr. Walton shouldn't operate on you?"

"Because, to put it quite simply, Dr. Walton is my daughter."

CHAPTER EIGHTEEN

CLINT FOUND HER hiding out in the attendings' lounge. The moment he walked in, carrying a tray of swabs and needles, she knew that he knew. Or at least Heidi had told him something.

It was the way the woman had looked at her.

That recognition.

And as their gazes had locked, that whole vivid memory of the night her mother had gone away played back through her mind, only this time her mother had a face instead of a flesh-colored blur.

"So this is where you've been hiding." Clint set the tray down.

"I haven't been hiding."

Clint shot her a look of disbelief and she rolled her eyes.

"Okay, fine, I was hiding, but I wasn't skulking."

"I was never going to suggest that." Clint sat down across from her. "So, she told me. Or she told me what she suspects."

"That I'm her daughter?"

Clint nodded. "I think you sensed something too."

"I knew the moment she told us her name."

"Do you want to do a genetic test?"

"Why?" Ingrid asked. "Does it matter? I know it's my mother. I don't need a genetic test, like some people I know."

Clint winced.

"Sorry," she mumbled. "I didn't mean it like that."

"It's okay, but you should do the test."

"Why?"

"Because if you're her daughter, you can't do her hip replacement."

"It's only biology that binds us, nothing emotional. My judgment wouldn't be clouded by anything."

"No, I wouldn't let you in there. You know you couldn't do it."

Ingrid stuck out her arm. "Then take my blood, Dracula, but be quick about it. I have a knee replacement surgery in an hour."

Clint pulled out the needle and began to prep the site. "Can you recommend a good ortho surgeon if this works out how I think it's going to work out?"

"McAdams is good. I would trust him." Ingrid winced as she felt the tiny bite of the needle. "Call McAdams."

"I will." Clint continued with his work. "Why did you run, besides the fact this woman we're treating is your mother?"

Ingrid shrugged. "Why don't you tell your parents you are back?"

"Are we really going to have this discussion here?"

"No."

Clint nodded. "Good. I'll have the results back for you very soon."

"Even if she's not my mother, I don't want to do the surgery."

"Why?" Clint asked. "Nothing would be stopping you then."

"Except me." Ingrid dragged her fingers through her hair. "If she's my mother then I'm going to have to deal with the pain of her abandonment. If she's not my mother I'm going to have to grieve over my mother's disappearance all over again, and I just can't handle that. Not right at the moment."

"I'm sorry you're having to deal with this."

Ingrid shrugged. "It's just bringing back a lot of stuff that I don't want to deal with. You know, once I thought I'd found her when I was about sixteen. I could've sworn the woman was the spitting image of me. I'd see her every day. She worked at a grocery store and in my mind I would fashion stories about how we'd meet again and what we would say to each other.

"I just built it all up and when my father found out what I was doing, he went ballistic. She wasn't my mother and my little bubble was shattered. It was the one thing that kept me going through my angsty teen years. The years when my father was trying to break my rebellious streak.

"Whenever I was feeling blue or down I could slip away into that fantasy and no one was the wiser. When that fantasy was destroyed, well, I stopped believing that I would ever find her. I'm not sure that I really want to at this point."

Clint didn't say anything to her. "We should have the results soon."

Ingrid nodded. "Look, don't tell me. Just...don't."

"I have to tell you, Ingrid. That's not something to keep from you."

"I would look into McAdams as soon as you can to do her hip replacement because, mother or not, I'm not dealing with those demons from my past today."

"Okay."

Ingrid watched him leave.

Even though she was trying to tell herself she didn't care if that woman was her mother or not, that young sixteen-year-old girl, or what was left of her, was excited on the inside.

Heidi Walton was her mother, but if for some reason

she wasn't, whatever was left of those childhood memories would die right alongside it.

Clint got a page from the lab and headed down to collect the results. When he got there, the technician handed him the piece of paper and he opened it.

Bingo.

Heidi Walton was Ingrid's mother.

He folded up the paper in his pocket and headed to his patient's room.

As much as he didn't want to divulge that Ingrid was his patient's daughter, Heidi Walton had asked him why he was doing the tests.

He could've lied and said it was a preoperative workup, but he followed a strict code of truth and ethics. There was no way he could lie. Not even for the mother of his child.

Or even the woman he loved.

And that thought made him pause before he entered Heidi's room.

Did he love Ingrid?

The very idea scared him, because he wasn't sure he was someone who could love. She'd worked her way past his walls last night, but he thought that was just lust.

It had to be.

Only he knew deep down he was falling fast for Ingrid. The woman he'd turned his mind to in order to escape the pain when he'd been tortured.

One of the strongest, most determined women he'd ever met.

Dammit.

How could he give love and be a good father when he couldn't even tell his own family that his tour of duty was over and he was back home, working and had a child?

When had his life become so messy?

That moment you let a blonde seduce you like a siren.

Clint shook his head, trying to clear the thoughts away. Right now he had a job and that's what he was going to do.

Heidi's head turned as he came into the room, the eyes so like Ingrid's tracking him across the room. "Well?"

Clint nodded. "You two are a match. She's your daughter."

He was expecting a gloat or something, but instead he looked at Heidi to see silent tears streaming down her face. She shook her head and then covered her face with her hand. Long slender fingers, like Ingrid's skilled surgical hands.

"Are you okay, Mrs. Walton?"

"I'm fine. You see, I knew I would never forget my Ingrid." Heidi brushed the tears away on the back of her hand and Clint reached over and brought her the box of tissue. "Thank you."

"Is there something I can do for you?"

"No, I don't think so." Heidi let out a long drawn-out sigh. "I've been looking for her for a long time."

"I thought Mr. Walton and Ingrid were from here."

"No, we're from Idaho. When my ex-husband tossed me to the curb and gained sole custody of Ingrid, he packed up their belongings and moved. He never told me why or where. God, that day almost killed me. I've been looking for so long."

"It was parental kidnapping."

Heidi nodded. "Only in those days that's not what it was called, and parental kidnapping was not a big issue. Not like it is today, that's for sure."

"It took you a long time to find her. Idaho isn't that far away."

Heidi sighed. "I know, but when you don't have money… when all you were was a housewife before your husband threw you out…it's hard to pick up and move, and in those days the internet wasn't around and I couldn't afford a private investigator."

Clint nodded. "The internet is a great thing sometimes."

"Almost a year ago I heard that there was an orthopedic surgeon in Rapid City, South Dakota. A young woman with blonde hair about the age of my daughter, and I knew I had to come here. I've been watching her for months, but I was terrified to approach her and…" Heidi trailed off and Clint's blood froze.

Heidi had been watching Ingrid for months, which meant she knew about Jase.

"Why didn't you approach her?" Clint asked, desperately trying to change the subject. Instead, it made the elephant in the room quite evident.

"She was pregnant. I didn't want to upset her or the baby." More tears streamed down Heidi's face. "Can you tell me what she had or, if you can't do that, can you please tell me that her husband is good to her? That she didn't make the same mistake and marry a controlling, manipulative man like I did?"

Clint bit his bottom lip. "I can't divulge any personal information, Mrs. Walton. I'm sorry. Truly I am."

Heidi nodded and then turned her head to look out the window. "I hope she didn't marry someone like her father. I hope she was able to choose her own path. My life was chosen for me for so long."

"She's one of the best orthopedic surgeons I've ever seen. I think she chose her profession and I know for a fact she loves her job."

Heidi smiled. "Thank you. Is Ingrid going to still do my surgery?"

"No," Clint said. "You're family. That's against hospital rules."

"So she knows."

Clint nodded. "She does. She recommends Dr. McAdams, another orthopedic surgeon, to do your hip replacement. We're contacting Dr. McAdams and he'll be in soon to discuss your surgery."

Heidi nodded. "Thank you, Dr. Allen."

Clint picked up Heidi's chart and left the room. He had to find Ingrid and tell her that her mother hadn't abandoned her and that she'd been looking for her for all these years.

That's if Ingrid would listen.

CHAPTER NINETEEN

INGRID WAS STANDING in the hallway and through the window she could see into her mother's room.

She was still having a hard time processing it.

Clint hadn't even said anything to her. He'd just brought her the lab results and left.

He hadn't had to. She'd known.

Dr. McAdams had been none too happy about being brought in on his day off, but once it was explained that Ingrid couldn't operate on the patient because it was her mother, he calmed down. Now Ingrid felt like everyone was staring at her, watching for her next move.

Judging her for not going to visit her mom or remain by her bedside.

All she wanted to do now was go home and hold Jase.

What a great way to ease back into work.

"Why don't you go in and talk to her?" Clint whispered in her ear as he came up beside her.

"What're you talking about?"

Clint cocked an eyebrow and clicked his pen. "You've been staring at that window for hours."

"No, I haven't. I've been charting." Ingrid sighed and then smiled. "I guess I'm having a hard time processing it."

"I understand, so why don't you go and talk to her"

Ingrid rolled her eyes. "And what should I say to her? 'Hi, Mom I don't really remember you, but how's it going?'"

Clint shook his head. "Maybe she has an explanation about why she hasn't been in contact with you all these years."

"Oh, yes? And I suppose she told you."

Clint put his pen back into the breast pocket of his lab coat. "She did."

"Are you going to elaborate?"

"No, because that would be violating doctor-patient confidentiality."

Ingrid closed the chart she was working on. "I have to go."

"Ingrid, you should talk to her."

"I have nothing to say to her."

And as the words slipped out of her mouth the alarms sounded for a code blue, from her mother's room.

Oh. God.

Ingrid tossed aside the chart and ran into her mother's room as the rest of the code team came rushing in.

"Don't touch her, Ingrid. You can't." Clint grabbed her shoulders and moved her to the side. She was simply a spectator as a team of her fellow doctors and nurses tried to save her mother's life.

Ingrid's throat constricted as she watched the proceedings.

Clint was in charge of everything as he examined her mother. Shouting orders as they worked over her.

The world around Ingrid was drowned out and everything seemed like a foggy blur, like she was watching a train wreck in slow motion.

"Ingrid," Clint shouted above the din. "She has an aortic dissection. We need to rush her in to surgery. You're her only next of kin."

Ingrid swallowed the lump in her throat. "Okay."

She couldn't lose her mother. She had so many questions. Why the hell had she hesitated?

Her father had told her for years that her mother hadn't wanted her. That her mother had walked out on them, but what if that wasn't true and now she was going to die?

"Prep an O.R.," Clint shouted. "She needs surgery, stat."

"Page Dr. Granule. I believe she's the cardiothoracic on call," Ingrid said above the din.

"Dr. Granule is in surgery," Clint said. "I've repaired an aortic dissection before."

The residents started moving her mother out of her room toward the elevators. Clint followed them and so did Ingrid.

Ingrid may have been an orthopedic surgeon, but she knew that an aortic dissection was a complicated surgery with a high risk of mortality, and Clint still had issues.

They got into the elevator and it whisked them down to the O.R. suites.

"I want a cardiothoracic specialist to repair the dissection." Ingrid stared at Clint. "Page anyone."

The elevator stopped and they pushed her mother to the O.R. while Clint headed into the scrub room. Ingrid followed him and watched as he peeled off his lab coat and put on a scrub cap.

"Didn't you hear what I said? Page someone else."

"I'm perfectly capable of performing an aortic dissection." Clint stuck his hands under the water and began to scrub. "I've done this procedure before."

"I want someone else."

"Why?" Clint asked. "I told you, I can do it." He put on a mask and headed into the O.R. Ingrid grabbed a mask and followed him.

"Because I don't trust you, Dr. Allen."

The scrub nurses turned and looked, and the anesthesiologist cleared his throat.

"Pardon?" Clint said as he stuck his arms into the surgical gown and then into the gloves. "What did you say?"

"I don't trust you." Ingrid glanced at her mother on the

table and tears stung her eyes. "You have PTSD, Dr. Allen. I've watched you freeze during a similar surgery not that long ago. You won't operate on my mother."

She was shaking as Clint's eyes darkened behind the mask.

What she'd said was horrible, but she was frightened. What if he froze when he was inside her mother and her mother died before she had a chance to find out anything? To learn the truth about what had happened between her parents.

"What?" Clint said, a cold tone to his voice.

"I want Dr. Granule. You know why."

She crossed her arms and stared him down.

"Dr. Allen, the patient is crashing," said a nurse.

Ingrid glanced at her and then back at Clint.

Clint moved toward her mother.

"Clint!"

He spun around. "It's Dr. Allen. Now get out of my O.R."

"Dr.—"

"Get. Out." And he turned his back on her.

Ingrid cursed under her breath and stormed out of the O.R. She was mad at the whole situation. Mad that she didn't trust Clint's surgical skills and mad at herself for not talking to her mother, but she had no one to blame but herself.

Because she knew whatever chance she'd had with Clint was gone.

She'd ruined it all.

Clint finished the aortic dissection repair. He glanced once up into the gallery and saw Ingrid standing there. Watching him.

In the O.R. it was tense. The scrub nurses were on edge and his resident asked more questions than usual; even the anesthesiologist was more attentive. As if they thought he was going to crash and burn.

Perhaps it was the hurt. The feeling of betrayal he felt at this moment that kept the demons of his past at bay.

Either way, he wasn't going to let Heidi Walton die on his table. He wouldn't give any of them the satisfaction of knowing he had failed.

"Dr. Hurt, will you close for me?"

"Of course, Dr. Allen." Dr. Hurt stepped up as Clint set down his surgical instruments and moved away from the table.

As he walked toward the scrub room he saw that Ingrid had left the gallery and he groaned. He didn't want to get into it with her again, but something had to be said.

She'd divulged his secret.

Word would get around and he could lose his job.

Though you shouldn't have been working.

He'd been cleared by the psychiatrists in Germany, but he was a good actor. He could understand her worry, especially since Ingrid knew what he was struggling with, but to announce it to the whole O.R. It could've given the surgery a really bad outcome.

She'd shaken the faith of his entire staff.

Ingrid came into the scrub room.

"Not here," he said, barely looking at her. "We won't discuss this here."

"Fine."

Clint finished scrubbing and moved out of the scrub room, Ingrid on his heels. He took her into consult room, flicked on the light and shut the door. He crossed his arms and leaned against it, staring at her.

"How did the surgery go?" Ingrid finally asked.

"Good. I was able to repair the dissection. Once she stabilizes, Dr. McAdams will be able to repair the damage to her hips."

Ingrid pursed her lips together and nodded. "What do you think caused the dissection?"

"Weakened tissue, and it was exacerbated by her fall." Clint scrubbed his hand over his face. "Is that all you wanted to discuss?"

"No. I'm sorry for what I did. I panicked."

Clint nodded. "You could've jeopardized the surgery. You do realize that? Everyone was on edge because of what you said."

"It was good they were on edge. They'd be able to pay attention in case you froze."

"You had no right to do what you did," Clint snapped.

"I had every right. She's my mother."

Clint snorted. "You could've fooled me because just before she coded you wanted nothing to do with her."

Ingrid's eyes narrowed. "She left me."

"She didn't leave you, your father kidnapped you."

Her eyes widened and she took a step back. "What?"

"I don't want to get into this with you, Ingrid."

Ingrid turned and looked away. "You don't know what you're talking about."

"That's what she told me."

"My father wouldn't have done that."

"Your father is a terrible person. Remember, I talked to him."

"Well, at least you talk to somebody's parents. You can't even talk to your own family."

It was like another slap across the face and he felt the walls going back up again. Why did he think he could let someone in? People couldn't be trusted.

People were horrible. Vicious and vindictive.

"I'm leaving now." Clint turned away from her.

"I'm sorry, Clint. This was all a bad idea."

He snorted and barely looked back at her. "You're telling me."

* * *

Clint wasn't surprised at all when he was called into the chief of surgery's office. It had only been a matter of time. Once other people in the hospital had legitimate concerns about the safety of their patients and the abilities of a physician in charge of said patients, well, Clint was surprised it hadn't happened sooner.

"Dr. Allen, come in." Dr. Ward motioned to the seat across from him.

It was just Dr. Ward in the conference room. No members of the board. No legal or HR person. Which meant he wasn't being fired.

Yet.

"You wanted to see me, Dr. Ward."

"Yes, your resident on your service this week, Dr. Haynes, had some concerns."

Clint nodded. "He's talking about what Dr. Walton said."

Dr. Ward nodded. "I'm a former army medic myself, Dr. Allen. Do you have post-traumatic stress disorder?"

Clint's blood froze because he didn't know what to say. For so long he'd kept the information guarded within him. Hidden from the world. He was so used to pretending everything was okay when deep down he knew it wasn't.

Who he'd been before his time overseas was long gone. Dead. The shell that remained behind had no feelings any longer and yet Ingrid had evoked some in him. She'd broken through the numb and anesthetized parts of him.

"I believe you have my medical records from the German hospital where I was transferred after my escape."

Dr. Ward picked up the file. "Yes, I have the reports here. They say you're cleared for surgery but discharged from active duty."

"Yes."

Dr. Ward's gaze narrowed. "Do you have post-traumatic stress disorder, Dr. Allen?"

"Yes."

A wave of raw emotion washed through him. It was so strong it overwhelmed him, but he kept himself together.

"I think you need to seek counseling, Dr. Allen. I know that Dr. Walton is…well, I understand it was her mother you were operating on."

Dr. Ward was trying to put it delicately that the whole situation was a mess.

"It's okay, Dr. Ward. I understand her concerns. She's right. There have been a few times when I could've potentially endangered my patient's life. The flashbacks have been increasing, but take a look at my track record. I haven't lost one patient since I started working here. My outcomes are good."

Dr. Ward nodded. "I know, but if the flashbacks are intruding then it's time to seek help."

"I know. That's why I would like to take a leave of absence to get this under control, if I may"

"That sounds like a good plan." Dr. Ward smiled and slipped him a card. "This is the hospital employees' psychiatrist and she specializes in post-traumatic stress disorder. I know because I'm a patient of hers. When I came back from overseas I had a hard time doing surgery because I would think about all the men and women who'd lost their lives during simple surgeries because we hadn't had the supplies or the ability to carry out the procedure safely. The ravages of wartime are not easily forgotten by those who live it."

"I was captured."

"I know, Dr. Allen." Dr. Ward tapped the report. "It's all in here."

"I have a hard time operating because I was forced to perform medical procedures on soldiers who were either tortured or wounded and didn't have anesthesia. It's hard to repair a spleen or cut off a limb while three other men hold the soldier down."

"I understand."

Clint ran his hands through his hair. "I thought about giving up my surgical practice and becoming just a general practitioner."

"But that's not what you want now?"

Clint shook his head. "I'm not sure what I want."

Liar.

He knew exactly what he wanted.

He still wanted to be a surgeon. He still wanted to save lives and make a difference, and he wanted Ingrid in his life.

Even if she hadn't believed in him today in that O.R., he could understand her reasoning. She may not know it but she was suffering the same way he was. Only she'd been suffering for a lot longer.

"Make an appointment with the psychiatrist and go down to HR and tell them you're on a medical leave of absence for a while. When Dr. Cleo gives you clearance, you can return to work. You're a damn fine trauma surgeon, Dr. Allen, and I would hate to lose you."

Clint stood and shook Dr. Ward's hand. "Thank you."

"Anytime."

Clint left Dr. Ward's office and headed down to the surgical floor. He had to find Ingrid. He had to talk to her and tell her what he was planning to do to help himself. He also wanted to tell her how much he loved her, but he couldn't do that.

The mere thought of it made him feel nervous and scared.

Coward.

He found her in the attendings' lounge. Her expression was unreadable and she was staring off into space. She didn't even look up when he walked into the room.

Dread knotted in his stomach.

"Did something happen to your mother?"

"No." Ingrid looked up at him. "I heard that you were called to the chief's office."

"Yes, he wanted to talk to me."

"I'm sorry."

"Apology accepted."

Ingrid nodded again. "Look, I think—I think you need some time to heal."

"What?"

"We've had a lot happen to us in this past year and I'm not ready for a relationship with you." She bit her lip. "Not until you get some help."

"What about you?" Clint asked. "What about you getting some help?"

"I don't have post-traumatic stress."

"I'm not talking about the PTSD I have, Ingrid, but you have demons from your past that you need to work on."

She nodded. "I know. That's why I think I should move out."

Clint took a seat. "Where will you go?"

Ingrid shrugged. "I'm off rotation for the next couple of days. I'm sure I can find a small apartment nearby in that time."

Don't let her go, his mind screamed at him. "Doris has been paid for the next few months, she'll be willing to go anywhere."

"Thank you." Ingrid got up to leave. "I should head back to your place and pack up my things and get Jase packed up."

Don't let her go.

"Okay, but leave a number where I can call you."

She paused. "Won't I see you at work?"

"No, I'm going on leave for a while."

Her face paled. "Oh, God, was that my fault?"

"Yes, but it's okay."

Don't let her go.

"I'm sure it is. I know how you felt about surgery." She waited, hesitating as if waiting for him to reach out and stop her, only he couldn't.

Don't let her go.

Her face was sad. "Goodbye, Dr. Allen."

Clint tried to move his body to stop her, but he was frozen. She left the attendings' lounge, closing the door between them, and he waited for the emotion to overcome him, but nothing came out. Inside his heart was screaming.

CHAPTER TWENTY

INGRID WATCHED THE interim head of trauma speak with her mother. It had been a week since she'd moved out of Clint's house and moved in with Phil.

Phil had an in-law suite above her garage that was currently empty and she'd gladly offered it to Ingrid.

Doris complained about the number of stairs up to the apartment, but that's all she complained about. Doris didn't say anything about Clint and Ingrid didn't either.

He was on paid medical leave, but no one knew for how long. When Ingrid tried to question Dr. Ward about it, he told her it was confidential information and he couldn't release it to her because she wasn't his wife, partner or significant other.

She was nothing.

She was the mother of his child, but that didn't get her anywhere and Clint hadn't been by to see Jase at all, which broke her heart.

She was a single parent. Even though she'd planned on parenting Jase by herself, it had been different since Clint had become involved.

Now she missed it.

Sure, he hadn't been very hands-on with Jase, but there had been times when he'd held their son or watched him while she'd snuck a bath.

He'd been someone to talk to at the end of the day.

Now when Ingrid came home and Doris left, it was just her and a chubby four-month-old.

And the cherubic four-month-old was cute to look at but she couldn't have a conversation with him.

She cursed Clint for coming back into her life.

She cursed him for making her fall in love with him, for needing him and relying on him, because she loved him. She loved him with every fiber of her being. She loved him and he'd left her.

Her father had raised her to take care of herself and be responsible for her own actions so she wouldn't be hurt like this.

Then again, according to Clint, what her father had been telling her all these years was a big fat lie. Now the only way to get any answers was from the person sitting in that room, recovering from an aortic dissection and a hip replacement.

The hip replacement had been done yesterday and she was recovering well. The aortic dissection was healing nicely too, though her mother still had a long road ahead.

Dr. McKidd came out of the room and Ingrid approached him.

"How's she doing?"

"She's doing remarkably well. We can most likely move her out of the critical care unit and move her up to the ward tomorrow."

"That's good," Ingrid said, and glanced back over at the room. Her mother was resting with her eyes closed, but somehow Ingrid knew she wasn't asleep. That her mother knew she was there.

So Ingrid took a step forward and paused in the doorway.

"You can come in, Dr. Walton." Heidi opened her eyes, eyes that Ingrid remembered with clarity. "I won't bite."

Ingrid didn't say anything as she stepped inside the room and shut the door. "How are you feeling?"

Heidi cocked her head to one side. "Are you asking me how I'm feeling as a physician?"

"No, because I'm not your physician."

Heidi nodded slowly.

"How long have you been observing me?"

"Not long. Only a couple of months. Is Dr. Allen your husband?"

"No, just the father of my baby."

Heidi chuckled. "I'm sure that thrilled your father."

"He disowned me."

Heidi sighed. "I'm sorry you had to grow up with him."

Ingrid shrugged. "I had no choice really. My mother was gone."

"Not by my choice, Ingrid. Never by my choice."

"I guess I'm having a hard time believing it when I've been told something different for most of my life. Why did you leave?"

"Because I didn't love him. Because he couldn't mold me the way he wanted me. I didn't want to live like that and I didn't want you to be raised like that either."

Ingrid sat down in the chair beside her mother's bed. "So he kidnapped me."

Heidi sighed. "Yes, only back then there was no such thing as parental kidnapping. He had sole custody and there was nothing I could do."

"You could've fought for me," Ingrid snapped.

"I had nothing. Your father took away everything. I had no schooling, no training. Nothing. I scraped enough money together to survive and go to school so that one day I could fight for you, but by the time that happened he'd sold our home in Idaho and moved away."

Her father had lied to her. All those years, telling her that her mother hadn't wanted her. That her mother had left them to live her own life.

That her mother hadn't loved her.

Ingrid dropped her head into her hands. "Oh, God."

"Did he tell you I didn't love you?" Heidi's words were choked. "I've never stopped loving you."

"I don't know what to believe anymore." Ingrid wiped the tears away on the back of her hand. "He always taught me that I wouldn't have help for the mistakes I made. That I had to accept my own consequences and it's what I've lived by, to not take risks, but it's…" She couldn't even finish what she was trying to say.

Other than she felt so alone. Like no one in the world loved her except Jase.

Yes, she'd made a mistake that night. She'd taken a risk and slept with a man. She may have chastised herself for doing it, for letting her judgement lapse, but she'd never regretted it.

Never.

"Life is all about chances, Ingrid." Heidi sighed. "I was young when I married your father. My parents were very much like him. They raised me to be respectable and play it safe. Your father was wealthy, handsome and I was a shy wallflower. When he paid attention to me, it was like I was the most beautiful girl in the world. We were married and he took me on a world-tour honeymoon, sweeping me off my feet and romancing me. It all changed when we got home. Life became dull and then I became pregnant with you."

"Do you regret that?"

"No, never. Only you weren't part of your father's ten-year plan for us. Still, he wanted to live up to his responsibilities and I was supposed to play the good housewife. Only times were changing and I was regretting the chances I didn't take. I started to go to school when your father wasn't around and I met a man."

"You cheated?"

Heidi's face fell. "I'm sorry, Ingrid. I didn't love your

father. I loved Patrick. He was just as destitute as I was. Only I could never marry Patrick because your father refused to give me a divorce before he disappeared."

"Where's Patrick now?"

Heidi's face fell. "I lost him to cancer about five years ago."

"I'm sorry."

"Don't be. I've known love, Ingrid. I've regretted a lot of things in my life—marrying your father, losing you—but I've never regretted having you."

Ingrid reached out and took her mother's hand. "Thank you for telling me."

Heidi took it.

Ingrid pulled out her phone and found a picture of Jase and passed the phone to her mother. She braced herself for rejection, for hurt. Heidi Walton was her mother, but they had no relationship. She could easily walk away after she was discharged. Heidi had made her peace and there was nothing keeping her from leaving.

Only something in Ingrid's gut told her that wasn't the case.

Heidi may not have been around for her childhood, but she could be around for Jase's.

"What's this?" Heidi asked as she took the phone.

"This is your grandson. Since Dad wants nothing to do with us, I thought that you might."

Heidi's eyes filled with tears as she stared at the picture. "What's his name?"

"Jase Allen Walton."

"He's beautiful." Heidi handed the phone back to Ingrid. "I would love to be a part of his life, but mostly I want to be a part of yours, Ingrid."

Ingrid bit her lip to keep the tears from flowing. "I would like that."

"So take some advice from me. Don't let Dr. Allen slip away."

Ingrid did a double take. "What—what're you talking about?"

Heidi rolled her eyes. "You've been taught to be self-sufficient and clinical, I can see that. I can see aspects of your father in you, but Dr. Allen loves you."

"How do you know? Did he tell you that?"

"No, he was very tight-lipped. Just as you are. You thought you were hiding from me in the hallway, watching me from a distance, but I saw you. And I saw the way you two gravitated toward each other. I saw the look in his eyes when he talked to me about you and when I told him what happened to me."

"He let me leave his house, though. He went on paid medical leave and I don't know where he is. I haven't heard from him and he hasn't been by to see Jase."

"You need to find him, Ingrid. Don't let him go. Tell him how you feel."

Ingrid let out a nervous chuckle and stood. "I don't know how I feel."

Heidi cocked her head to one side. "Don't you? Search your feelings."

"I'll see you later." Ingrid opened the door and left her mother's room. Her head was whirling and she was trying to process everything.

Did she love Clint? Really love him?

Yeah, she did, but she was terrified of letting go of that control over her emotions, of allowing someone else in her life.

It was a scary prospect. It would be a challenge to overcome, and since when had she ever backed down from a challenge?

She took an early lunch. She ran out into the parking lot.

Glad that it was a mild, clear day and the roads wouldn't be slick.

It didn't take long for her to get out of the city and onto the highway. Even though she hadn't driven this way in two weeks, the route was familiar to her.

Her heart felt like it was going to leap out of her chest by the time she turned down Clint's road and her pulse thundered in her ears when she saw his ranch house. As she pulled up the long drive, something wasn't right.

The door opened and his maid, Maria, came out of the house. Ingrid approached her.

"Maria?"

Maria turned and grinned. "Ah, Dr. Walton. It's good to see you again. How is that adorable baby?"

"Jase is good. Doris takes excellent care of him."

Maria smiled. "I'm happy to hear it."

"Where is Dr. Allen?" Ingrid could barely get the words out of her mouth as her throat was constricting and her heart was racing.

"He left to visit his family, I believe. He left a week ago."

"Do you know where he went?"

Maria bit her lip. "I think he went to Bismarck. I think that is where he said his family had moved to, but I'm not sure."

"Do you know when he'll be back?"

Maria frowned and gave her a sympathetic look. "No, he did not say when he was to return. I drive out once a week to clean, but I haven't done shopping for him in a while."

"Thank you, Maria."

"He said he'll phone me next week. Do you want me to pass on a message?"

"Just tell him that—tell him I dropped by and that the baby is doing well."

Maria smiled. "I will. Good day, Dr. Walton."

Ingrid's stomach sank to the soles of her feet as she

headed back to her car. She realized that Clint was gone and there was no guarantee of if and when he would be back.

He hadn't left her a number where she could contact him, which meant he'd probably washed his hands of her and Jase.

Which meant he didn't feel the same way as she did.

And it broke her heart, but what could she possibly expect?

The man had been damaged by war. He'd warned her in the beginning that he had nothing emotionally left to give her, but she'd continued on with him.

That night he'd come to Jase's room and told her that he wanted her, she shouldn't have given in to him. She should have stopped him.

Except she'd wanted him too.

So badly.

Now it was gone and she had no one to blame but herself.

She'd embarrassed him in the O.R. She was the reason he'd had to go on medical leave.

If she hadn't been so crazy, if she had spoken to Clint about her concerns privately before he'd stepped into the O.R., then none of this would've happened.

You did the right thing.

That's what she kept trying to tell herself. That she had done the right thing. His post-traumatic stress disorder had the potential to put a lot of patients at risk.

Still, she wouldn't blame Clint for hating her.

That's why she'd moved off the ranch. So she wouldn't have to deal with his cold looks and awkward silence.

Besides, he hadn't exactly tried to stop her from moving out. He'd let her go.

What was she thinking about, driving out here and declaring her feelings for him? He paid Doris, so he knew where she was.

His actions spoke volumes and she was an idiot for driving out all this way because she'd let her emotions get the better of her.

It hurt, but she would get over it. She had to for her son's sake and for her own healing.

This was why she'd never wanted to get into a relationship in the first place. This was why any relationship she'd had in the past simply hadn't worked.

Only you pushed them away.

And she had, because she'd been guarding her heart. Then she couldn't hold back the tears any longer. They began to flow freely, so she pulled her car over to the side of the road at a rest stop. She was thankful she was alone in the car to let out everything she'd been bottling up.

She cried for her mother, she cried for her father and most of all she cried for her son, but none of the tears were for her, because she didn't deserve them.

It was her fault.

And she deserved everything she got.

The only one who would suffer here was Jase and that broke her heart.

She didn't want to be on the same level as her father. She didn't want to deny Jase his father, but she'd done that with her idiotic actions.

When she was finally able to regain control of her tears, she dried her face with a tissue and took a few deep breaths before she even contemplated getting back on the highway and heading back to the hospital.

Ingrid hoped one day that Clint would heal enough to come back, but she wasn't going to rely on that flimsy dream.

She loved Clint and always would.

A man incapable of returning her love. A man who, even though he was claustrophobic, had so many walls guarding his heart that she couldn't even begin to contemplate breaking through, but you couldn't help who you fell in love with.

That was a cruel twist of fate.

As she'd been taught her whole life, she'd live with the consequences and take responsibility for her own mistakes, so when Jase grew old enough to ask about his father she'd tell her son that it was her fault he was gone.

And probably, when that day came, she was positive that she'd lose Jase too and that thought scared her to her very core.

CHAPTER TWENTY-ONE

Two weeks later

CLINT STOOD OUTSIDE Philomena's house. Actually, he stood outside Philomena's garage and stared up at the apartment above it.

Courage.

This was scarier to him than joining the army and going overseas.

He'd left Rapid City a month ago and hadn't told Ingrid where he was going or what he was doing. Though Maria had mentioned to him that Dr. Walton had been by the ranch two weeks ago and he was kicking himself for not calling Maria sooner, but he'd been busy.

He'd been dealing with his PTSD and part of that healing process had been to go and visit his family. Which had been difficult.

So difficult.

His father had never wanted him to join the army and he had certainly never wanted him to go to medical school and become an army medic. He'd wanted him to go into construction, with him, but Clint had wanted to be a doctor.

When he'd been captured and tortured, he'd lost his love of practicing medicine and in his mind he could hear his father berating him. Clint had felt guilt, because he no longer wanted to be a surgeon but also because he'd thrown away his chance to be a part of his father's legacy.

All this guilt was eating away at him inside.

He'd had a hard time going back to his family. He had struggled to deal with what he'd seen as failures instead of what they actually had been—setbacks.

Hiccups in the road.

When he'd shown up on his mother's doorstep, it had been a shock to her.

"Clint?" He could still hear the shock and the joy in his mother's voice as she'd wrapped her arms around him and held him close. Then the questions had come and a few cuffs to his head for not telling them sooner that he'd come home.

When he'd finished explaining it all, his mother had held him again.

Told him that he had nothing to feel guilty about. He'd done his duty, as well as he'd been able to, and for that his father would be proud.

That his father had been proud of his surgeon son and that he had been proud that his son had gone into the military and that he might have to go overseas one day to save the lives of soldiers and insurgents alike.

And then Clint had broken down and told his mother about everything he'd been through, including Ingrid and what had transpired between them.

How he'd ruined it because he couldn't open up emotionally to the woman he loved. The woman whose faltering and fleeting memory from their one night together before he'd been shipped out had got him through so much.

There were times he wondered if he loved Ingrid only because her memory was like a safety blanket, but he knew that wasn't true.

When she'd told him she was moving out and taking

Jase with her, a part of him had died, only he hadn't had the emotional strength to reach out and take what was his.

He was a coward and he was still working on forgiving himself.

It was his mother who had talked him through his feelings. And when his mother had found out she was a grandmother and hadn't known about it, well, that had earned him another cuff to the head.

His mother had actually come down to Rapid City last week to see Jase and Ingrid, and had met Ingrid's mother too.

When Clint had asked his mother if Ingrid had asked about him, his mother had said she had, but only to make sure he was okay.

And that stung, but what did he expect? He'd let her go and hadn't told her he was leaving town.

He'd severed all ties with Ingrid and Jase.

And he was regretting it now, because he wanted them to be a part of his life and he wanted to be a part of theirs.

He wanted to be the kind of man Ingrid deserved. Even though he had a long way to go, he wanted Ingrid and his son by his side.

Leaving her and letting her go had been the stupidest mistake of his life. One he aimed to rectify.

Even if she pushed him away, he was going to stay close to them.

He was going to return to work. He was going to earn back Ingrid's love and trust.

There was no one else for him.

All that mattered to him was Ingrid, Jase and becoming a surgeon again. He was going to beat the PTSD and bury the demons of his past, because they were just ghosts.

He was tired of living in the shadows, of carrying around a haunted past. All he wanted was a bright future.

One full of hope and healing.

With a deep breath he climbed the stairs up to the apartment and knocked on the door.

Doris came to the door and her eyes widened when she saw him. "Dr. Allen, what a pleasant surprise."

"Hi, Doris. Is Dr. Walton in?"

"No, she's at the hospital, but she should be back in an hour." Doris stepped to one side. "Would you like to come in?"

"I would."

As he ducked under the shorter doorframe he realized how cramped this new apartment was and he didn't like it one bit. His fight-or-flight instinct kicked in, but he closed his eyes and counted to ten and got control of the fear of being in a confined space.

"Are you here to stay, Dr. Allen?"

"For a while."

"Well, if you don't mind I need to run down to the store and get Jase some more diapers. May I leave him with you?"

"Of course." Though his heart began to race at the thought of being left alone with his son. It had been so long since he'd seen him.

Doris smiled. "I'll be back in half an hour."

Clint nodded as Doris left the tiny apartment.

He was left alone, standing in Ingrid's tiny living room, which was a mishmash of seventies and eighties decor. It looked like some old lady's apartment and he knew it definitely wasn't Ingrid's style.

As he peered out a small window to watch for Ingrid he heard a cry.

Jase.

Who was supposed to stay sleeping until Ingrid came home, but, then, babies didn't really conform to schedules.

Clint headed down the hall and found Jase's door and opened it.

The first thought that struck him was how much his son had grown in a month. He was lying in his crib, his little fist curled as he rubbed his eye, sniffling as he did and probably smearing snot all over his chubby cheeks.

Tears stung Clint's face and he regretted having missed a month of his son's life. Actually, he'd missed out on more because he'd been so emotionally detached from life for so long.

He wanted to go in and comfort him, but he was also terrified because he didn't want to scare his son. He was a virtual stranger to the boy.

Coward.

He took a step forward and the floor creaked.

Jase's head swung around and Clint was met with two clear blue eyes, and it was like he was looking at himself in a mirror.

Jase's lip stuck out as he pouted and his eyes squinted as he let out another pitiful cry. Clint didn't want to scare him but he also didn't want to leave him here alone and crying.

"Hey, big guy. Don't cry." He moved to the side of the crib and picked Jase up, holding him close. Jase only let out a few small hiccups as Clint bounced him gently in his arms. "Don't cry, your mom will be home soon."

Jase stared at him. His eyes were wide and he reached out with one damp, wet, curled fist and touched his face, smearing drool and who knew what on his cheek.

And then he smiled and gurgled. A great big toothless smile that warmed Clint's heart, and then Jase lay his head against Clint's shoulder, right under his chin, as Clint swayed back and forth.

How stupid he'd been. He'd almost lost all of this because he was an idiot.

Even if it didn't happen today, he was going to make

amends with Ingrid because he wasn't going to let her or Jase out of his life.

There was a small snore and he realized that Jase had gone back to sleep. Gently he placed his son back in his crib and then backed out of the room.

All he wanted was Ingrid and Jase.

All he wanted was his family and he was going to make sure he got it.

Ingrid pushed open the door to her apartment. She was running a bit late, but not that much. She set the chicken dinner she'd bought to go on the counter and realized the apartment was eerily quiet.

"Doris?" Ingrid called, but she got no answer. Confused, she set down her purse.

As she walked to the living room a man materialized from around the corner and she let out a small cry and covered her mouth.

It was like a ghost from her past was standing in her living room.

All six feet of him, clad in a black leather bike jacket, jeans and a dark T-shirt. He looked well rested and had filled out a bit. He resembled the man she'd slept with almost a year ago. The soldier who had gone off to war.

"Clint?" she said, finally finding her voice.

"Hi, Ingrid."

Tears stung her eyes and her body began to shake as she looked at him "What're you doing here?"

"I've come back to town."

"I can see that, but what're you doing here?"

"I've come to see Jase." He ran his hand through his hair. "I've come to see you."

Her heart skipped a beat. "Me?"

Clint took a step forward. "Yes, you."

Ingrid's body began to shake and she suddenly felt nervous so she took a step back. "I don't understand."

He grinned, those blue eyes sparkling. "You don't understand?"

"You left!" Ingrid snapped, finally finding her bearings again. "You left us without so much as a word as to where you went."

"I know," Clint said. "And I regret that, but you moved out. I could say the same thing about you."

"Did you honestly expect me to stay after the fight we had?"

"No, I don't blame you for leaving." Clint took another step forward. "I wasn't emotionally there and I was hiding. I was afraid and I used what happened to me to keep people out because I was terrified of feeling again. Emotions were used against you in the prison I was held in. I learned to bury them. I just hadn't realized how deep I'd buried them."

Ingrid nodded. "I understand. I wasn't imprisoned in quite the same way, but I was taught not to have emotions. I was raised to be clinical about everything so that when I had no control over my emotions because of the pregnancy I didn't know how to handle them. When you bottle things up for so long..."

"They explode." Clint smiled. "I've missed you and Jase and I regret every day we've lost."

Ingrid quickly wiped away the tears that were threatening to spill. "So you went to see your family."

"I did. I believe my mother came last week."

"Yes! Thank you for the warning."

Clint chuckled. "I didn't know until after she'd come here. My apologies. I would've got a message to you. Would you have denied her her grandson?"

"No." Ingrid smiled. "She was sweet."

"She told me I was an idiot."

Ingrid grinned. "Well, now I like her even more."

They both laughed at that.

"So you've come to be a father to Jase?" Ingrid tried not to sound too eager, she didn't want to push Clint and scare him off. She liked this side of him and she wanted him to get better. She didn't want to be so emotionally closed off. Her son deserved his father.

"If you'll let me."

"Of course. I would never deny my son his father."

Clint nodded. "He's not the only reason I've come back."

And then he stepped closer, closing the gap between them, and Ingrid found her knees knocking together again as she stared up at Clint towering over her. She could smell his cologne and it made her blood heat.

She longed for his arms to wrap around her and hold her close, to kiss her, to possess her, because he was the man she loved.

And then he did reach out and touch her, the pad of his thumb brushing across her cheek in a gentle caress that sent a current of electricity and passion through her body.

"I came back for you."

"You did?" A tear rolled down her cheek. "I—I don't know…"

"Ingrid, I know I don't deserve your love, but I do love you. You're the one I want to be with and I don't blame you if you can't return that love because I blocked you out for so long, but I want you to know how I feel about you. I can't live without you and I will wait for as long as I have to to have you back in my life."

He hadn't abandoned her. He'd come back, which was hard to come to grips with because this was not what she'd been taught to believe.

Ingrid broke down in tears. The ugly crying, big large ugly sobs as everything she was feeling came out.

Clint pulled her close. "Shh, it's okay. It's okay."

Ingrid shook her head and pushed out of his embrace. "No, it's not."

"I told you, I understand if you don't—"

"Shut up. I love you, too."

Clint's eyes sparkled and he smiled. "You do?"

"Of course. I went out to the ranch over two weeks ago to tell you that, but you'd left. I love you, Clint. Only you. I didn't want to, but I can't help it. I love you. Always and forever."

And before she could say anything else, she was crushed against his chest, his mouth claiming hers in a passionate kiss that scorched her very soul.

How could she have thought that she didn't want this? This was all that mattered. Jase and Clint were all who mattered in her life.

She couldn't live without Clint.

She didn't want to.

When the kiss ended he held her close and she held him tight, worried that this was all a dream.

"So, how long do you think it will take you to pack, and will Phil need some notice before you move?"

Ingrid chuckled. "It won't take me long to pack. All of my furniture except for the crib is still at the ranch."

Clint grinned like a Cheshire cat. Smug and self-assured. "Good. Pack your bags because you and Jase are coming home with me tonight."

"Gosh, what will Phil say? I signed a lease in blood." She winked.

Clint chuckled and pulled her back against him. "Marry me, Ingrid. Tomorrow."

Clint leaned in again to kiss her, but they were interrupted by a shout in the other room. "I think our son would like your attention now, Dr. Walton. Shall we go and tell him the good news?"

"I don't think he'll understand."

"But we'll tell him all the same, won't we?"

Ingrid grinned. "Yes, Dr. Allen. Oh, yes."

Hand in hand they walked to their son's bedroom to cuddle their son together. As well as pack so they could start their life together right. For the second time.

Only this time would be the last and would be forever, because Ingrid knew that this love would last and she would only love once.

Forever.

* * * * *